HOME IS THE HEART

HOME IS THE HEART

a novel by
Roberta Gibson

Afterword by
Brooke Medicine Eagle

BEAR & COMPANY
PUBLISHING
SANTA FE, NEW MEXICO

Library of Congress Cataloging-in-Publication Data
Gibson, Roberta, 1958-
  Home is the heart.
  I. Title
PS3557.1224H66 1989   813'.54 88-33297
ISBN-939680-64-5

Copyright © 1989 by Roberta Gibson

All rights reserved. No part of this book may be reproduced by any means and in any form whatsoever without written permission from the publisher, except for brief quotations embodied in literary articles or reviews.

Franz Kafka's poetry is reprinted with permission from *The Great Wall of China: Stories & Reflections* by Franz Kafka, translated by Willa and Edwin Muir, copyright © 1970, published by Schocken Books/Random House, Inc.

Bear & Company
P.O. Drawer 2860
Santa Fe, NM 87504

Cover & Interior Design: Kathleen Katz
Cover Illustration: Vinaya Wall
Editing: Gail Vivino
Typography: Buffalo Publications
Printed in the United States of America by R.R. Donnelley

9 8 7 6 5 4 3 2 1

*In Loving Memory
Of Our Sister
Cynthia*

Contents

Acknowledgments ix
Poem: "Footprints" x

Chapter One 1
    Two 9
    Three 15
    Four 19
    Five 25
    Six 31
    Seven 37
    Eight 43
    Nine 53
    Ten 59
    Eleven 67
    Twelve 73
    Thirteen 85
    Fourteen 91
    Fifteen 101
    Sixteen 107
    Seventeen 117
    Eighteen 123
    Nineteen 133
Starting Your Own Moon Lodge 141
Afterword 149
About the Author 157

Acknowledgments

This book could not have been written without the support and love of many people. My first thanks goes to the Creator and the inspiration to write this story. Secondly to my husband Larry, and our children, Jinji and Ola Faye, for their loving support; to the many members of the Four Winds Family (too numerous to mention) for their united vision; to the computer wizardry of Terry Cook and his gracious family; to the many women who organized and participated in the Moon Lodge ceremonies; to Mary Ellen Carlow for her editing advice; to my Mother and Father for nurturing me; to the staff at Bear & Co. for a job well done and a pleasurable publishing experience; and last, but certainly not least, I am thankful to have had the honour to experience the courage and extra ordinary strength of Cynthia Thekan, as she dealt with cancer and the threat of life and death. It was her beautiful heart that allowed this book to be created.

Footprints

Footprints
    empty, hollow soles
Tread lightly to fill vacant holes.
Much too large, they sink
    unsure
Is this the only way?
Father's blessing path
    a journey traveled for years untold.
One more heart
    will view the symphony
    of ancient
    combined minds.
But, alas
There must be something new,
These footprints wide and worn
    leave little promise to unsung lives
    but more to growing old.
Now, even tho a different trail
    is dense and unsurveyed
It is surely fresh and new
    with secrets that have yet to be
    derived, discovered, from their depths
    overflowing, bountiful detour
Leaving new footprints for souls of brave
Summoned clear of well-worn roads.

Chapter One

A crackling fire, a booming drumbeat, the rattle of a bean-filled gourd — each sound was amplified by the intensity of the mood. Five women sat, hand in hand, forming a circle with the presence of their bodies. From within them, a deep sound arose, as if from the depths of the Earth, starting slowly and soon escalating to a high pitch. In rhythm they chanted, over and over, the song of the Earth and the sky. They brought the spirit of balance to their lodge.

Slowly their feet began to move to a beat that was unfamiliar to their heads. It was a strong and pounding dance, full of the rhythm of their ancestors. They moved in harmony, letting the energy of the moment carry them in motion. Then, ending suddenly and spontaneously, all five slouched to the damp, sage-covered earth. Charged by the song and dance, their bodies trembled and they gasped for breath as the fervor of their desire brought its results: a spiritual release.

A hollow, wooden bowl of water was raised to the heavens by one of them and a humble prayer of thanks was delivered as each woman hungrily slurped the wetness as if it were the first or last drink she would ever have. Another hand revealed a fist of myrrh gum, and with the confirmation of its powers, sprinkled it carefully over the embers of a now dying fire. The sweet, pungent aroma filled their heads with visions of mystery and richness.

Another woman reached for a stone, a palm-sized, smooth rock that seemed to hold secrets it might never share. It was the prayer stone, and it had been witness to many solemn vows and commitments. It was now part of every prayer it had ever heard, and was treated as such. The keeper of the sacred stone issued a call to start the prayers.

She began, "O Father Sky, Mother Earth, Creator of all life, we give thanks for this day and this power that has brought us together in this holy lodge. For those who have mothered and come before us — grandmothers, mothers, the gentle co-creators of life — may the wisdom of your years be upon us. Our hearts are filled with joy at the beauty that surrounds us: the trees, the flowers, and the sky. For the winged ones, the four-legged and the two-legged, for our relatives who swim the oceans, we are forever grateful. May we learn to respect all life, every insect and being, for they are of your making. Thank you for blessing us with a home to live in, food to eat, clothing to wear, and fresh air to breathe."

A deep sound of approval was released by the other women with a "HO!" that seemed to echo forever. The keeper of the stone continued, "I would like to say a special prayer for our sister, Cynthia, who is on the other side of life. May the union of love that we feel here tonight fly like an arrow, swiftly to her heart, bringing her strength and light. For our friends and family, and all the little children who dwell on the Earth, may they each be blessed with peace and understanding so they may achieve their dreams.

I ask for mercy for those who are hungry, sick, or in need. Send them hope. For myself, I ask only for guidance to be able to serve the Creator and humanity in a positive way. Inspire me.

"For all we have, again I give you thanks and praise. I am forever grateful and filled with humility at the abundance life holds before us. Make us worthy of it. May peace prevail on Earth. My sisters, my friends."

She then passed the stone on to the next in line, a hand that reached out in the darkness. This woman, and then each woman after her, shared her thoughts and prayers, her vows and feelings of hope and purity. As the stone circled, each heart swelled with satisfaction and a knowing that all goodness, peace, and truth can be found in the spirit we each hold. Each eye swelled as well, with tears of thankfulness and honor at being part of such a ceremony. As the stone was passed to the last woman in line, she shared a closing prayer, completing the circle; all hands were joined tightly. The ritual formed a deep and lasting bond, and each learned much from listening to the others' prayers.

Then they began to breathe. A firm and steady in and out, they synchronized the beating of their hearts. In harmony, they shared the sacred air of life. They created such a oneness, such a union, that their prayers rose together as one to the etheric realms above. As in a trance, the women's breath was transformed into a chant, a long and joy-filled chant, shrouded with gratitude:

Earth my body, water my blood,
Air my breath, and fire my spirit.

> Earth my body, water my blood,
> Air my breath, and fire my spirit.

More herbs were tossed on the fire, bringing slight hints of perfume to the air. Then, in a clockwise direction, they followed each other out of the wooden, six-sided lodge into the moonless night. A mountain chill was in the air, so they huddled together, formed a circle again, and began to sway back and forth. Clapping their hands, they created a slow and steady beat. Facing left, they began another dance, circular in motion, each foot stepping twice. They squatted every few steps to touch the firm, precious Earth. As they revolved, they sang:

> The Earth is our mother, we must take care of her.
> The Earth is our mother, we must take care of her.
> Hey yunga, ho yunga, hey yung yung.
> Hey yunga, ho yunga, hey yung yung.
> This sacred Earth we walk upon, with every step
>   we take.
> This sacred Earth we walk upon, with every step
>   we take.
> Hey yunga, ho yunga, hey yung yung.
> Hey yunga, ho yunga, hey yung yung.

After four rounds they suddenly stopped, faced each other, and, as if they all heard the same call, released a shrill, piercing scream which was sent to the heavens and crumbled the solitude that surrounded them. With this scream of release and recognition, they let their guardians know that they were finished.

Hugging each other silently, the women departed, each returning into the world to try and keep the intensity of purpose that she had assumed in the lodge of the sisters. They would come together again when the moon was new, to refresh themselves in spirit and to renew their commitment to each other, to their Creator, and to themselves.

▶ ◀

She left the lodge, a young woman now, unburdened by her prayers. She had seemed to age quickly as of late, and the relief she felt from the ceremony was pure peace. Into the late model Volvo she hopped, taking a deep breath and relaxing into the seat. Carefully working her way down the mountain in the darkness, her thoughts were filled with the destiny she had created for herself. She wondered how she had let it get so far out of hand. The sickness had progressed so slowly, unnoticed day by day, and now she was dying. My God, she thought, we never appreciate life until it's saying goodbye.

Her thoughts were instantly disturbed by a dark flash in the corner of her eye. Thump! Whatever it was bounced off the windshield. Slamming on the brakes, she slid off the side of the dirt road. She gripped the steering wheel tightly, her eyes on fire, and tried to calm her heart, wondering what she had hit. Apprehensively, she creaked open the car door and stepped out to see the form of a bird lying in the dirt, barely illuminated by the glare of the headlights. It was a large bird, she noticed, as it attempted to flap its right wing with little success. Realizing that it was seriously hurt, but not dead, she considered her options and decided that her only choice was to bring it home with her. It was too late to take it anywhere else and she certainly couldn't just leave it in the middle of the road.

"You poor thing," she told the bird, in the most comforting voice she could muster, "I'm really sorry. God, how did I manage this one?" She rubbed her forehead. "Well, uh, let's get you in the car. Just take it easy; this isn't going to feel real good."

She brought a blanket from the trunk of the car and, with a large stick she found on the side of the road, gently rolled the feathered creature onto it. The bird released a high squeal, at which the woman jumped back in fear. Heart pounding rapidly, she took a deep breath, gathered up the blanket, and lifted it, amazed at its lightness. She laid him on the back seat, wedging him between a suitcase and a pair of boots. She knew that if anything was broken it was best if he remained as still and quiet as possible. In the light of the car, she got a closer look at him. "An owl!" she softly whispered to herself.

There seemed to be no external bleeding, at least as far as she could see, but tears of remorse filled her eyes as she wondered if he was dying. Quietly she mumbled a simple prayer for the motionless bird and realized that she would have to get him examined in the morning.

Pulling herself together, she began winding her way along the miles of hills and curves to her home. Her thoughts were filled the whole way with images from the strange night and with the powerful peace she had felt after the ceremony. How easily that peace had been disrupted. She wondered what was to become of her relationship with the injured owl and the healing they both needed to live.

Chapter Two

She awoke with a start, emerging from a peculiar dream. It had left her with a haunting feeling that raised goosebumps on her skin in the chilly morning air. Remembering the owl, she glanced over to where she had laid him the night before. He was gone! Her stomach dropped. Grumbling, she slid into her slippers and stumbled from her bed into the living room. First she looked up in the rafters of the old cabin, hoping the bird had recovered and had flown up there. There was no sign of him, so she continued searching and finally spotted him hiding under a chair. She crouched down to peer under it and the owl, trembling, cowered in fear, cornered and full of despair.

"Well, at least you are alive," she told him, relieved, and gave him a gentle smile to let him know he was safe.

Suddenly, she remembered last night's dream. While setting out some water and bread crumbs for the bird, the memory of it persisted.

▶ ◀

The dream had seemed to last all night. As it began, she found herself in a meadow, bright sunlight streaming through the trees and a creek gently winding its way down the hillside. The colors seemed vivid, almost alive, and wildflowers were scattered in every direction for as far as she could see. Feeling very content, she lay down on the tall, green grass and hummed a tune. It must have been midday, as the sun was high overhead. The air was so still she could hear her own heartbeat, and deep inside herself she gave way to the contagious harmony of nature, breathing fully and with release.

At the peak of this absorption, she heard a voice, wispy and gentle, but forcefully deep. "The wind is the director of life. Bend with us; do not resist."

She sat up with a start, eyes darting about, trying to find the owner of the voice. Again, she heard it. It was the grass! It was speaking. The blades were all talking, echoing the message, over and over, like a hundred tiny voices whispering together. Then they stopped, as suddenly as they had begun, and she found herself wondering if she had really heard anything at all. Feeling a little crazy, she repeated the message a few times so as not to forget it, and then stood up to shake off the feeling.

Dazed and deep in thought, she began working her way down through the meadow when she was startled by a long, brown snake that circled her feet as she stepped. Clockwise, it moved as she did, either slowly or more quickly, depending on her pace. She began to alter her steps, first to the right, then to the left a few times, hopping and skipping, keeping no pattern. The snake anticipated her every move, and the two of them began to dance in an uneven sort of polka, leaving trails of crushed grass behind them.

Mesmerized by the weaving motion, she barely noticed

when the snake slithered up and wrapped itself around her right leg. She shook her leg, thinking she was tangled in the grasses, and gasped as she peered down to find the serpent spiraled about her calf, its little snake tongue darting back and forth towards her knee. She froze, panicked and fearful, and stared into the creature's eyes. It spoke to her, roughly and slowly, as if its forked tongue were in the way. "Hold on tight to life, and feel our Earth Mother beneath your belly as I do. She will heal your pain." Then, with a nod of its head, it unwound itself and gracefully slithered off behind a large rock.

Unsteady and dizzy, she drooped to the Earth. Her mind was spinning, trying to make sense of what had just happened, and she felt tears running down her face. The tears were not of sadness, but of total relief and gratitude. The fear she had felt towards the snake was the fear she felt towards her own death, and the shock of looking it in the eye was almost more than she could endure. Was life really so fragile, she wondered?

Feeling a slight chill, she observed that the sun was not overhead anymore. A few clouds had moved in and were blocking its warming rays. The sky seemed to become darker, taking on a 'before storm glow.' Then she became aware of the rock that the snake had slid under. It had changed. It was glowing, an ominous sort of glow, which was there and yet not there — a bluish tint in its aura.

Wiping her tear-streaked cheeks, she sat up, confused. She tried to prepare herself for what would happen next, hoping not to be caught off guard again. Cross-legged and patient, she waited for what seemed like hours, yet only minutes actually passed. She stared at the rock, and lost herself in its brilliance. Its swirling colors, blending and changing, denied the rock's density, and she felt drawn to them. Hypnotized, she felt as if she were a rock, firm and solid, and she became aware of a glow about her own body. She was the Earth, rooted firmly in its ancient secrets, transformed by wisdom. Patterns of twirling light surrounding her, she could see her own colors: greens, reds, and hints of purple, like tiny vortexes engulfing her presence and being. When she became aware of the rock again, she could feel little distinction between it and herself. They blended into one; no boundaries existed, and they breathed and pulsated together in harmony.

"Sit in silence and observe as I do. All things you need are within." She did not know if she was speaking or if it was the rock. Her head began spinning with the words 'within, within' until she lost contact with everything.

Moments later, she opened one eye and found herself sprawled out in the grass again, shaking. That was intense, she thought, wondering if she was herself. She regained her senses and looked over to the rock. It was a normal rock by all means, motionless and quiet, no glow, no nothing. I have lost my mind, she decided, and she stood up and stumbled over to the creek.

As she splashed her face with ice cold water, she massaged her neck unconsciously and glanced toward the sky. A large bird was hovering above, its graceful wings spread out, waiting for the next breeze. Suddenly a shot rang out! The bird flapped jerkily and quickly fell to her feet with a loud thud. She jumped back in surprise and observed that it was a beautiful brown and gray owl, now wriggling in pain. Gasping, she turned quickly away. Then, compassion replacing shock, she turned again and bent down to stroke him and ease his discomfort. He tried to resist, squeaking strange sounds and pecking at her hands, his talons lashing out. Then his head dropped and he fell into unconsciousness.

She scooped up the bird into her arms, folding his injured wing gently under his limp, motionless body, and began walking down the creekside in search of help. Feeling calm and determined, she whispered words of love and comfort to this creature that was a stranger to her. She said a simple prayer, asking for guidance, and squeezed her eyes tightly closed to dispel the tears that had filled them again.

▶ ◀

That was all she recalled as she awoke to find that the owl she had hit with her car was nowhere in sight. Her heart beat excitedly as the memory of the dream made its impact on her real world, and she stretched out on the couch to discover her owl shyly picking at the bread crumbs she had left out. Trying to make sense of it all, scenes and words flooded her mind, and she tried to determine if this owl was the same as the one in the dream. She decided he was.

What did it all mean? What did she have to learn from all those strange messages? With a deep urgency, she told herself that she must take good care of this owl and keep him alive and healthy, as he had a message to share with her that might be the key to unlock the solution to her own health. Of all things! she thought. An owl to be my teacher. Well, things could be worse.

"Let's get you to a doctor," she told the owl, and prepared to leave.

Chapter Three

She had left Denver three months ago, in the spring of the year, a confused and tired woman, sick with cancer. They named it Hodgkin's Disease and gave her one year to live. She was prescribed everything from sedatives to chemotherapy, and began treatment with reluctance. She knew that it was only for a matter of time that the drugs would keep her alive. They were not really healing her.

A lot of physical pain filled her body, but the worst pain was in her heart. Emotionally she was a wreck. It all made no sense to her. Friends and family treated her so differently, as though she were some kind of lost stranger that they had compassionately taken into their homes. They were too nice, and this made her illness even more unbearable.

She tried to keep her job so that the insurance would cover her medical bills, but her ability to function sanely in a stressful occupation waned quickly. Ironically, she was a nurse.

Her whole life seemed to fall apart in a month. Depressed and lonely, she contemplated suicide. She felt as if she might as well die, as she could find no valid reason to live through all the pain. Death seemed more real than life now. She became obsessed with it, and wanted to deeply understand what was going to happen to her. Between treatments she roamed libraries, bookstores, and schools, searching for details or information that might shed even a small ray of light on her demanding questions. Death was something she had never considered much, as she had been eager just to live. Now she stood face to face with it, in fear, and in shock.

Her family began worrying about her. Her doctor suggested she see a therapist. The pressure was on and she knew she was losing control. She felt surely that life had more to offer her. There were so many more things she wanted to do. Her time couldn't be up yet. There had to be more.

She knew she had to get out of the city, and go someplace where there was peace and quiet. Someplace where she could think. The city would be an ugly place to die, amidst concrete buildings, honking cars, and flashing billboards. How could she ever hope to understand what life, or death for that matter, was really about in this steel jungle?

I must escape, she decided, considering her options on where to find that elusive element, solitude. She recalled a small family cabin up in the mountains where she used to go when she was a child. It was a special place full of fond memories and she had always loved it there. The air had always been so fresh, and she could remember the long morning walks with Grandfather in the forest. He had shown her many beautiful places. These places were their secret spots, and they had placed piles of rocks along the trails so that they could always find their way back home. In the evenings they would sing songs around the woodstove, and Grandfather would make up incredibly tall tales that never ceased to put her into a deep slumber. The memories were pleasant ones. It was the one place she could think of that brought her visions of solitude.

Since her Grandfather's death five years ago, no one had spent any time at the cabin, and she felt a twinge of remorse that she hadn't made the effort to go up to the mountains lately. But now the cabin held a very different and essential purpose for her life. She could just go up there and die. No more treatments, no more job, no more struggle. Comparatively, her life would be insignificant, but peaceful.

Relieved that she had finally found a way out, she began to plan her final journey home.

She talked with her Grandmother and parents regarding the condition of the cabin and found that the house was still set up for use. They thought the journey and the mountain air would be good for her, but they advised against a long stay. It was heated only with wood and they felt it was much too rural for a sick woman. They anticipated the worst. She was insistent though, and reluctantly they gave her the keys, silently hoping that she would not stay too long. They understood her desire to escape and the passion she had for the mountains, but they felt that her only chance was the treatments and the safety of the city. They underestimated her newfound devotion towards a genuine tranquility.

After packing the items to be left behind, she stored them in the basement of her parent's house, where she had been staying to ease the financial burden of her therapy. She informed her doctor of her decision, much to his dismay, and she also told her friends, who had trouble supporting such a risky venture. She closed all her accounts and finished all her personal business. Focusing on these trivial things kept her mind off thinking about what the next few months would be like, but she wanted to leave nothing undone since she felt she would not be returning.

She packed her car with a small parcel of belongings — clothes, blankets, writing material, some food, and other essentials she did not want to have to buy. She gathered up a few favorite books and the savings that she had set aside, a sum she hoped would last at least six months. She didn't require much to survive.

Satisfied that she had everything a dying woman would need, she began her journey westward, breathing more deeply than she had in months.

Chapter Four

 Morning sun cascaded into the kitchen windows as she fixed a large breakfast, famished by last night's adventures. She was in a hurry to get the owl to the veterinarian's office, but decided to take time to eat and spend a few extra minutes with him so that he would feel more at ease with her on the ride to town — if that was at all possible.

She coaxed him out the door to sit in the sun with her. When she offered him bits of pancake, however, he just ignored her and tried to waddle off. He didn't even attempt to flap his wings, so she knew that he had sustained a dangerous injury. She did not want him to leave, as she was sure he would die out in the woods without being able to fly, so she got up to block his way with her body. He attempted to create paths around her but finally gave up the game, frustrated and trembling, and strutted under a lawn chair to hide.

She sat down within view of him and, contemplating his stately posture, decided he should have a name. He was mostly brown with some interspersed gray feathers, and a dark tail. His most amazing feature was the white area around his eyes. It was almost heart shaped and stood out brilliantly, framing his wide, questioning owl eyes. He stood about twelve inches high, and was presently so still he could have been a statue.

Between bites of pancakes she tried out different names, and finally settled on Harris. Not Harry, mind you, but Harris, a name she thought symbolized stature and respect since, of course, owls were very respectable creatures. It had been the name of her maternal Grandfather, whom she had loved dearly, and it was he who had built this cabin. He had had a deep respect for nature and the name seemed appropriate. Happy with her decision, she cleaned up breakfast and prepared to leave.

Even though it was traumatic for Harris, she had to use the old blanket trick to get him in the car again, but she kept him by her side for the whole ride, singing old childhood lullabies. It probably didn't help the bird, but it kept her calm.

The veterinarian was surprised at their arrival but, to her relief, admitted them quickly. After an examination, which included injecting a sedative into the owl (owls are very tender hearted and die easily from fright) the doctor determined that there were not any internal injuries. He said the wing was not completely broken but simply fractured and he would have to splint and wrap it. She helped steady the bird while the doctor wrapped a piece of cloth around the properly positioned wing. He told her to keep the bandage on for three to four weeks, after which it could be removed, but if the owl was not yet able to fly, she should bring him back in. The doctor then suggested that she take the owl to the zoo for proper care and feeding, but she declined, knowing that he did not belong in a cage for the rest of his life.

She thanked the doctor for his help and advice, wrapped the still drowsy owl in the blanket, and headed out. The ride home was uneventful and gave her time to think. She realized that she would have to care for Harris until he was well and could fly again, and she was pleased to have the honor. She would make him a little house, keep him inside at night, and do some research on what owls eat. It would turn out to be a real learning adventure.

She built him a large wooden cage that she referred to as a roost, which was solid about the edges and open at the top. Filling it with soft, green grass, twigs, a few insects, and a small bowl of water, she wondered how she would get Harris into it. She found a pair of old, leather gloves used for tending the woodstove and approached him to try and pick him up. Harris eyed her suspiciously, as if he knew exactly what she was thinking, tucked in his wing feathers and backed up a few steps. This isn't going to be easy, she thought. She spoke quietly, trying to coax him with gentle sounds and words. She assured the bird that she would not hurt him, but he seemed not to believe her and retreated two steps for every one that she took. Then, lunging quickly, she circled his feathered body with her hands. He squawked loudly, attempted to flap his wings, and pecked at her gloved fingers. She took care to escape the clutch of his quick-moving talons, as they were razor sharp.

Surprised at his strength, she struggled to maintain her grip. Adrenalin pumping and breathing heavily, she placed him gently into the makeshift cage. She removed her hands, and he unruffled his feathers and stepped about indignantly, head thrown back, beak up.

"Sorry about that, Harris," she said, and laughed at

his obvious, but comical, distress. It was then that she knew they were to be the best of friends.

The days passed slowly and Harris progressed well. She didn't want to stress him by taking him in and out of his cage, so she just brought the roost in at night and left it outside during good weather. It was large enough for Harris to walk around in, but he mostly kept still and quiet trying to adjust to his new conditions.

She researched an old herb book that was in the cabin's library and found that comfrey tea was a good healer of broken bones, so she gave him that instead of water. He soon regained his strength and she became fascinated with him. Watching him prune his feathers, meticulously cleaning each one, she wished he would not be so afraid of her. She wanted him to trust her.

One day she brought him outside to clean his cage. She had found it a difficult thing to do, especially while wearing leather gloves, with Harris backed into one corner, his eyes strangely unfamiliar. When she was finished that day, she offered him a piece of apple, her hand held out stiffly until she felt as if it would fall off. She was just about to give up when his beak reached out, then darted back, then reached out again and pecked a small piece of the apple from her fingertips. Amazed, she tried to stroke his smooth feathered head, but he had had enough for one day, and jumped back defensively, leaning on his back, talons poised dangerously.

We're slowly making progress, she thought as a twinge of pain struck her chest. "You'd better get well soon," she told him, "because I may not be able to take care of you much longer." Stretching out under a cloudy sky, tears of sadness filled her eyes.

Chapter Five

 The first night that she arrived at the cabin was filled with a curious fear and confusion. She had gotten lost on the way up, and it was a dark and rainy night.

Searching for the cabin's fusebox, so that she could turn on some lights, she tripped over a chair and fell sideways into the woodstove. Moaning, she released a long wail of frustration, wondering what she had gotten herself into. She was scared, lonely, and not sure she could pull it off. She wished it were over — that she were already dead. Her fear turned into anger at the predicament she had to deal with, and the anger gave her a certain strength. Pulling herself up off the floor, she trudged back to the car. She unrolled her sleeping bag on the back seat, climbed in exhausted, and slept there for the night. She would deal with the cabin tomorrow.

Even though it was already early May, mornings came late to the canyon and the sun was barely over the ridge when she awoke. Emerging from the car, hair tousled and back aching from the cramped quarters, she stood in awe of the scene that surrounded her. Never before had she remembered it being so beautiful.

There was an early morning orange glow on the upper rocks of the canyon that sent shadows into the sunken crevices scattered on the cliff-like walls. Last night's rain had not yet dried, and tiny raindrops glistened in the sun's rays. Everything was so green! All the trees — scrub oak, pine, and cedar — seemed to dance in the gentle breeze which caressed her face and hair, and melted last night's fear. She felt refreshed.

The cabin stood amidst it all, square and bulky, a little out of place in the gentle lines of nature. It was built in the lowest part of the canyon in a small flat meadow down by the creek, nestled among a large stand of aspen trees that thrived on the river bed. Grandfather had built an oversized deck on the front of the house facing west, as he loved to sit there and watch the sunset. The cabin was made of logs, housed two fireplaces and a pitched roof, and was well built and insulated, though not very modern. There was electricity, but no phone. The plumbing was old and the house was heated only with wood, cut from the many acres of forest around it.

The sun peeked over the ridge, signaling the day to start, and bringing her out of her trance. Happy to be there, she whistled a familiar tune, stretched her hands to the sky and smiled. Things looked better today. She walked over to the house to continue her search for the fusebox. What a mess! Cobwebs were everywhere, an ancient dusty smell hung in the air, and the murky windows let in a stingy bit of light. A mouse scurried across the floor in front of her and she jumped back in surprise.

Looking around, she decided it would take a full week to get the place together. She finally found the fusebox and, unpacking her car, began organizing and cleaning the place she would call home for the next twelve months.

As time went by, daily habits and rituals were formed out of need and a true desire to fully explore herself and her new environment. She became an early morning riser, practicing yoga exercises every day at sunrise that she had learned years ago, but never used. She wanted to find out what it felt like to do things she had always wanted to do, or to do the things she just thought she should do, but had never taken the time for. She would spend the later morning hours reading, walking, or just thinking. Many days she would silently sit and gaze out the window at the incredible scenery. The front porch became her bedroom and on warm, windless evenings she and Harris would bathe in the moonglow while they slept. Well, she slept, but Harris, being a night predator, loudly whoo-hooed at every forest noise. The deep sound of his owl voice lulled her in and out of sleep all night like the waves of an ocean roar. The stars became her companions, and many a night she made a wish on them for the future. She figured if the stars could be so amazingly beautiful, and if there were galaxies upon galaxies up there somewhere, then there had to be some hope for a simple being like herself. She felt insignificant, but not alone, as her delicate wish floated up to the perfection of the universe. It was so inspiring to her.

At times she felt very sick and depressed, and she would have to rest, nausea and headaches overwhelming her. At other times she would get bursts of energy and go outside to cut wood or repair things that were falling apart. She knew her Grandfather would be proud of her. Winter was not far off and she wanted to be prepared as much as possible, as she knew that she might be very weak by the time the snow started falling. The summers here had always seemed so short and the winters too long. She was now on her own, and the nesting instinct was settling within her, for, she thought with a chuckle, she surely didn't want to freeze to death while she was dying.

Finding an old hand-saw in the shed, she cut off the lower dead branches of elderly pine trees and other evergreens, and stacked them next to the house by the back door. They were not large pieces — mostly kindling — but at least she would not have to split any of it. Though it was hard work, she was not a frail woman, and soon acquired a good-sized pile. It felt good to be outside working, and soon she found herself talking to the trees and apologizing for taking their branches. It was a curious sort of exchange, but she truly felt as if they were talking back to her. Not with words really. It was more an unspoken communication, and eventually she just thought her words to them, rather than speaking. If she concentrated on one tree long enough, it would tell her stories about the past, and how it felt living there, and how it was happy to give her wood to keep her warm. She was not sure if it was her imagination or not. Her mind could be playing tricks on her but, nonetheless, it kept her occupied and content to think that, besides her starry friends in the night sky, she had a few down below as well. She wondered if she was losing her mind, and decided it didn't much matter.

She made lists of everything she would need to do: sweep the chimney; buy plastic to cover the wood and the windows; and buy prepared, non-perishable food, hearty boots, and some essentials for the house. She took an inventory of the cabin and found, to her surprise, that most of the things that she needed were there. Dishes, pots and pans, candles, blankets, soap, lightbulbs; someone had been prepared. It was a blessing for her. She had a lot of work to do, but she was determined, and usually by the end of the day she was so exhausted that she would just nibble at a little dinner and be asleep by sunset. Early to bed, early to rise — this had never been her lifestyle before. Living in the city, life was so different. Survival had been reduced to daily work in a large building and going to the supermarket. One turn of the faucet for hot water, a turn of the dial for heat, another for air conditioning, a flip of the switch for lights, a zap in the microwave for an instant dinner. How far away from Earth I've gotten in the last ten years, she thought. I worked a stressful job all day to earn enough money to pay someone else to supply all my necessities, rather than doing it myself. Why does it seem so strange now? It all seemed so normal last month.

    She felt a chill rush through her, raising goosebumps, and realized that a lot of things were going to be different as she spent more time alone and began to really think about life and its purpose. It was so quiet: no phone to ring, no television to watch. She was used to being distracted a lot. The stillness held no secrets. It exposed all thoughts and all truths by its very nature. It was her mirror and it scared her a bit, for she had never before seen herself so clearly. In her mind, childhood memories filled the house, and although it made her feel irresponsible and playful, it also proved to her how much she had changed and how old and stubborn she had grown. With no husband and no children, her heart had crusted over and become numb. She was not sure she liked the reflection in the silent mirror.

Feeling a little fear and apprehension beginning to creep into her mind, she reassessed her goals and set her mind on changing. She needed to keep it together a little longer so that she could die, prepared and in peace. Strangely enough, dying no longer scared her. It was the living that worried her the most.

Chapter Six

"I'm off to town, Harris," she told the sleepy owl, blowing him a kiss. "You just stay here and keep an eye on the place." He responded by blinking and adjusting his feathers.

She drove down the winding, dirt road, out of the canyon, and headed for the library. She was worried about Harris and wanted to do some research on owls. He was not eating what she was giving him. Also, he seemed rather lethargic and no longer put up a fight when she tried to stroke him. She figured he was probably very unhappy with his living situation, but he was not ready to return to the wild and she could not stand the thought of taking him to the zoo. She decided to attempt everything she possibly could first, and then consider less desirable options.

Harris had been with her almost ten days now, and she had grown quite attached to him. She put a lot of energy into taking care of him, which allowed her to keep her mind off her own problems. The waves of loneliness that she had experienced prior to his timely arrival seemed nonexistent now. The bird somehow filled her mothering need, and her friendship need. He was the companion she would never have consciously sought out. He helped to open her heart.

Driving into town now and then had turned out to be

an uncomfortable journey. When she entered the small community, she felt like a stranger in a strange land, as she didn't know anyone in town. It was always noisy and busy, a pace she had come to dislike, and she usually found herself wishing that she were already on her way home. She had become so accustomed to being alone in the last two months that she was not sure the hermit part of her could ever return to living a city life. Solitude had become her close friend.

Reaching the library on this particular day, she parked and hurried in, as she didn't want to leave Harris alone at home for too long. She located the information and began to browse through the books that looked interesting. The library was calming to her, and she felt more relaxed here than in any other part of town.

She recalled that the library was where she had met Ginger, the woman who had invited her to the Moon Lodge ceremony. She had overheard two women discussing the ritual and had bravely inquired as to what they were talking about. She was usually not so bold, but they had seemed very friendly, and as the conversation had continued, she had ended up sharing with them almost her whole life's story. They had told her that the ceremony would probably be very helpful to her, and that while it might not heal her body, it would give her spirit the strength and guidance to make the right choices.

Ginger had explained that the ceremony was developed out of the women's need to join together on the Earth and pray for things that were very important to them. They felt that the combined effort could be more effective than individual prayer. The new moon emphasized fresh beginnings to them, so they chose that day to get together. The ceremony was organized prior to their arrival. Preparation and organization had become the keys for a successful ceremony, although the format allowed for spontaneity and individual expression. Ginger had explained that every person was involved and responsible for a certain part of the ceremony, with no one person in charge. The ritual was not a true American Indian Moon Lodge ceremony — that was just the name that they had bestowed upon it because the moon influenced them greatly. It had evolved into a sort of support group for women, with a great concern for each other's processes. They respected each other's dreams and encouraged attentiveness to each individual's highest light. Every lodge focused on a different theme, like world peace, so that all thoughts were united towards one purpose for greater power. Ginger had told her that the upcoming lodge would be on "healing our hearts" and it had seemed so timely for her that she had asked if she could be included. They had welcomed her with open arms and she had felt as if this were the start of something wonderful, as if she had been in the perfect spot at the perfect time.

Returning to her owl studies, she felt a warm glow in her heart recalling her Moon Lodge adventure. It had truly shown her that there were other people around with ideas and visions similar to her own. These folks seemed more like relatives than her own family, and she felt a renewed confidence in her dreams, knowing that others were working towards the same goals.

She found a book that had been written by a family

who takes in injured wildlife, and they had a whole chapter on caring for injured owls. She learned that owls are usually very shy birds that don't like to be stroked or held much, and that they are very prone to heart attack from shock or fear. This didn't surprise her much, as Harris didn't like to be handled either, but she felt lucky that he was still alive after all he had been through. The book suggested that the bird be kept quiet and still in a wire cage large enough to flap his wings in. Her roost was a little small by these standards and she tried to envision, in her mind, what the revised cage would look like. She also found out that owls eat at dusk — mostly rodents, frogs, small birds, or insects. They are true carnivores. For the care and healing period, the book suggested, rather than trapping the owls' food, buying raw beef heart or liver and feeding them this. The birds thrived on fresh kills, but in the intermediary crisis period, beef hearts would suffice. The thought of feeding Harris raw hearts was nauseating to her, but she was much relieved to find that she didn't have to trap any rodents. She was willing to do whatever it took, though, to keep this bird alive long enough to heal itself and be set free. The food must have been one of the reasons for Harris' lethargy, as, in her ignorance, she had been feeding him fruits, grains, bread, and leftovers. She had had no idea about his wild diet and the doctor had told her little about his care. No wonder he wasn't eating.

Another book put out by the Audubon Society described the many varieties of owls in North America. She had never realized there were so many — over hundreds of varieties — each with different habits and lifestyles. They ranged from dwarf owls, that were six inches tall, to the average-sized barn owl, to a large species with an incredible wing span, standing twenty inches high.

Harris was a Montana Horned Owl, strong for his size, and she was glad she hadn't hit a larger owl. With all the information she had just acquired, she was satisfied that the veterinarian had done the right thing by wrapping the injured wing. She determined that it would take anywhere from ten days to three months for Harris to be able to fly again. It all depended on the severity of the break. She had opted against x-rays at the veterinarian's office, so only time could tell, and she would just have to "wing it" in the meantime.

She laughed to herself. She wished that Harris was the one winging it, not her.

Collecting a few books to check out, she left the library and went to the market to buy Harris his dinner. It was a small market, unlike the incredibly massive ones of the city that she always got lost in. She found the beef hearts to be inexpensive, so she purchased a large quantity. She would freeze the bulk and then would not have to drive to town every other day.

She was glad she had done her homework. Being responsible for another being's life was a sacred duty, and she wanted to do a good job and be successful. She wished deep inside that she had someone to take such good care of her: to tell her to eat the right foods, rub her feet, and tuck her in bed. Even though it sounded like it, it was not a mother she was hoping for. She was a grown woman and had normal desires like all others, but in the past ten years she had stayed away from all men as if they were poison. She did not want to get involved now, fall in love, and then die. Her heart was a tender one.

Chapter Seven

The pain was bad. She had woken up feeling nauseous and by midmorning it had gotten worse. She could not hold down any food. She lay around the cabin, changing positions every few minutes, uncomfortable and very unsettled, unsure of what she was doing. Dying wasn't as easy as she had hoped it would be. Nothing helped to ease the pain. Foolishly she had left her medication in the city, and there was no one to talk to, no escape from the intensity.

Lost and lonely, even Harris's antics couldn't cheer her up. She began to cry, longing for relief, sadness rising up from deep inside her being. Shivering with grief, she felt sorry for herself. What had she created? Must she take responsibility for this ruined life?

Claiming ignorance, she realized she was a wreck and that she had failed. Wasting away, day after day, she had not paid attention to what was really important — she had been concerned more with her next paycheck than the destruction of the Earth, more with personal pleasure than the suffering of her neighbors. She denied herself a good time — real recreation — to sit in front of the endless entertainment of the T.V. Ironically, she had become one of the victims she viewed daily. The aura of the city had smothered her and she had let it.

Another wave of tears flooded her eyes as she realized how tragic this was and how many others were doing the same thing. What a waste! How had she let it get so far out of hand? She had really lost perspective. She was dying.

NO! she thought, I am not dying, I am killing myself. Just as we are all killing the Earth. Just as we kill animals to eat them. Feeding Harris last night, she noticed how he had torn into the meat with true delight, his carnivore instincts relishing in the blood of the kill. He was a natural sanguinary creature. If I had to attack an animal myself, she envisioned, and kill it, skin it, take the guts out, cook it, and then enjoy eating it, I would feel as if it were right. Just as Harris had done. But the thought was revolting. Completely disgusting.

She was appalled and shaken to the core. No wonder I am dying, she thought, I am eating death. Dead blood and muscle. Another wave of nausea shook her body again. How peculiar it all suddenly seemed.

Unconsciously eating what I have been given, she theorized, I never really thought about what I was doing. I've been brainwashed all these years into eating this 'great protein' seductively wrapped in neatly packaged cellophane and plastic dishes. The notion was unbelievable. This is not the reality of death, she thought, it has been made so easy, so accepted. All those poor little critters, being raised only for slaughter, without hope of ever growing up to see the sun shine. Insensitivity at its peak.

She continued to feel worse.

Well, that's it, she decided, no more dead meat for me. I must change my ways. This idle consciousness of mine is going to start to occupy my mind once again. I am dying, quickly, and there is nothing I can do about it, but I will not take any more living creatures with me. I will live the rest of my days as peacefully as I can.

And she had fortitude.

I might as well begin taking responsibility for my life now, because I never have before. I've always blamed doctors, my parents, my job — the fault was always theirs. My life is my own responsibility. It's not their fault I am dying. It's mine. I created this. I have been so blind, but the past is the past and I cannot change what has happened. But, I can change the future.

Drying her tear-filled eyes, she closed them and spontaneously began to pray. "O Creator, I am in so much pain. I have created a miserable existence for myself, a reality that is distressing and dismal. Please help me to appreciate my life before it is gone. I am weak, but firm in my convictions. Guide me to help the Earth and the animals and my brothers and sisters. Forgive me for my mistakes, before it is too late."

With this, she burst into tears again, tears from her heart, tears of release and hope, healing tears.

A good cry always calmed her, and although she was tired, the pain appeared to be much better now. Stepping out of the womb-like cabin into the sunlight, she felt instantly charged and decided to go for a walk. She followed the creek up the valley, walking slowly, breathing deeply, taking in all the beauty that surrounded her. She wanted to absorb every minute of it.

The rocks seemed so overwhelming, shimmering in the

light, looking as if they had been purposely carved by hand. They outlined the canyon as it weaved its way through the hills. It was a dreamy place, full of wildflowers and tall grasses, aspen trees shaking in a gentle breeze. The creek was good-sized and ran all year round from the constant, high mountain runoff. The snow-capped mountains were visible from most of the canyon, especially from the cabin, but once one followed the creek to the end of the canyon, the high rock walls disrupted the view.

It was in the darkness of the canyon's end that she had first seen the cave in which she used to hide during her childhood summers. It was a craterlike hole that was cut back into the rock wall for about twenty feet. She never took any member of her family there, but rather used it to write and dream and feel special. There was always something magical about caves to her. It was as if she were seeing into the Earth's heart, a den of security and mystical secrets. In the dimness of the interior, she could make out veins of quartz and mica that lined the walls. Her most secret dream was that she had discovered gold and would someday use its riches to save the world. Very lofty goals for a girl of thirteen.

As the memory faded, she walked by a small waterfall that drowned out her thoughts. She bent to fill her hands with cold, fresh water and caught a reflection of herself in a calm pool near the shore. She looked good for her 34 years, but her usually long brown hair was short now from the chemotherapy treatments. Quite a definite change, though, from the young girl who used to gaze in these waters years ago. She felt older than her days, and the young, dancing eyes were now dull. They were still curious, but harbored a sadness that made them droop at the sides. Her youthful tan was gone, and her pale skin had a puffiness that she seemed unable to give up.

Not really liking what she saw, she turned quickly and sat down in the green grass near the creek to take in the view. Her self-consciousness diminished as she turned her thoughts to the spectacle that lay before her. Nature seemed so in tune. How did it know when to do what? It never made mistakes: the leaves always dropped at the right time, the sun rose and set perfectly on schedule. It had a rhythm she had lost.

Feeling awkward and clumsy amidst all this perfection, she wondered how a God or a Creator could foster such incredible feats every day for thousands, or even millions, of years. The magnitude of the idea eluded her reasoning capacities. Exhausted with her contemplation of life, she lay down and closed her eyes, sinking into the comfort of the Earth's carpet. It felt so peaceful, so relaxing. She breathed in the sweet aroma of wildflowers and drifted off to a place just between sleep and daydreaming, satisfied and finally smiling.

Chapter Eight

The Moon Lodge had been a wonderful experience for her. Never before had she heard women, or any people for that matter, pray so benevolently and purely. They had a real purpose in mind, and it wasn't just to save themselves. They seemed more concerned with the problems of others than with their own. This alone caused her to have a great amount of respect for the women and their ceremony.

The lodge had satisfied a deep spiritual need within her that had previously been difficult to satisfy. When she had gotten sick she had begun to pray every day to a God she was not sure even existed, figuring it was better late than never.

Her parents had suggested that she attend church services with them, but she had not really felt a part of the ritual. She had felt so useless just sitting there. The sermon had been inspiring at times, but it had seemed to her that the audience had listened, nodded their heads in agreement, and then had walked out the door and forgotten it all. How many had really gone out and helped the poor? How many had really felt that their neighbor was their brother? And how had she managed to be the odd one, the one with the unfortunate fate to question this age-old system?

She had decided that most of them donated their

hard-earned money so they would be saved. So, when the basket had passed her way, she had put in a lot, hoping somehow that if she paid God enough money He would heal her. Hey, money was that important to everyone else! But it didn't work, and she had felt ripped-off, as if she had been tricked by some invisible, mysterious, hooded savior.

The system had failed her and she had felt there must be more — something more real and tangible that she could relate to — but she had not been sure where to find it. The community had offered little in the way of support to spiritually undernourished residents who were dying. She was on her own.

Moving to the mountains had been her savior. Hearing the two women at the library talking about the Moon Lodge had hit her like a bolt of lightning. This ritual had been unlike anything she had ever heard of. It had seemed a realistic approach: the women created their own ceremony — they were the ceremony! Each person was involved. Their church was the Earth, the castle of God's own making. It had been a way and she had had to check it out. It had sounded real.

Attending the ceremony, she had cried as she had listened to the other prayers. They had been so honest and from the heart. The women had prayed to a Creator that they really believed in, that made a difference in their lives. They saw their Creator in nature, in people, and in every experience that happened. Everything and everyone was sacred to them, down to the tiniest insect.

These women also lived what they prayed! Their strength was in helping others, in living in harmony with their surroundings, and in a deep faith that was rooted firmly in their hearts. There was one thing that she felt was the most important: they were each so sure of what they were doing, and they trusted the processes of their lives so completely, that each experience was a growing one, a reminder to pay attention and change. They trusted themselves as well, so that each followed her own inspiration, or highest light, to direct her on her journey, rather than relying on the wisdom of a priest or someone else. Each of them realized that her chosen lifestyle allowed her to be open to her spirit, and that her spirit knew what was best for her. Direct inspiration allowed these women to be responsible for their own choices and to better learn from their experiences. It was not as if they never discussed problems with others, for they supported each other immensely; it was that they were accountable enough to be their own judges and juries. Very humbly so.

She had not felt as if there had been any physical healing for herself, but in her heart and spirit she knew that she had changed. There had been some sort of spiritual rejuvenation. And, although she didn't realize it at the time, the healing of her spirit was the first step on the long road to regaining her body's health.

To have found something to believe in was more than she could have asked for. It gave her the hope she had never known. And she knew now that even if she died, she at least would have found some peace.

She decided that the purpose of life is to grow, to learn and experience, to help others, and to enjoy. Nothing else. This was a great realization for her. She had always thought that life was to get rich, to stay young, to succeed.

I've been brainwashed again, she said to herself, by some sick, perverted idea that I must compete and be better and younger and richer and smarter than everyone else. Unconsciously I have played that game. What does all that matter? Aren't we here to love each other? Our society has lost perspective. My God, she thought, I have to let others know this. I can't die yet, there's news to spread! I must find a way to convey this information. I must show people how they are wasting their lives on unimportant things and getting sick in the meantime. They are dying without knowing what happiness really is.

She felt enthusiastic, and more concerned than she ever had. She now had a purpose. Satisfied that she had finally diagnosed the dilemma of the world, and that she had something important to share, she eased quickly into her world liberator role and fantasized about where to direct her ramblings.

Then she remembered a woman at the Moon Lodge ceremony talking about an all-night vigil that she had done. It was called a vision quest. For four days and four nights the women had sat and prayed and fasted to receive guidance and pay homage. She wondered if she had the stamina to do that. It might be just what she needed to give direction to her newly formed purpose. She would have to call Ginger tomorrow.

▶ ◀

The next morning, as she was getting ready to drive into town, she had a happy realization. As she combed her close-cropped hair, she noticed that it was beginning to thicken and grow in. She felt prettier now than when she had caught a glimpse of herself in the creek. She began to put on her makeup and then stopped with a frown, realizing that she was still playing the 'young and pretty' game and that she didn't actually need these chemicals on her face. She looked fine without them. She only put the stuff on when she was going to town anyway. She washed off the makeup, feeling a bit naked but relieved, and knew she would get used to it in time. Change wasn't easy, but it seemed that it was becoming her new profession.

Grabbing a glass of juice, she walked over to the roost and found Harris perched on a piece of wood. She no longer kept him in the cage all the time, as she felt like it was a jail and realized that Harris was not guilty of any crime. She was the one who had run into him. He finally seemed able to enjoy his new surroundings, and she always kept the roost open when she was home. Rather than rebuilding it to suit the guidelines of the book she was researching, she just hinged one side and made a makeshift door. She could not envision any cage being big enough for him, and the house seemed to serve the same purpose. The only real danger to Harris was being outside, unprotected and disabled.

Allowing him free reign also had its benefits. Harris, being a night predator, had solved the mouse dilemma she was having. The mice had become accustomed to having the cabin to themselves in the last few years, and had nested in almost every wall. This was not something she was very happy with. They were constantly startling her and they got into the food and cupboards. They were a real nuisance. She was against using live traps or poison, and was at a loss as to what to do, when she noticed that the population seemed to be decreasing quickly. She had never actually seen Harris catch one, but one night she heard some noises while she was in bed — mouse squeakings and wings flapping — and figured it out for herself. She looked for remains in his roost, and was surprised to find nothing. It was an unexpected bonus to having a live-in owl that she had not considered.

The raw beef-heart diet must have been just what Harris needed, because he seemed to be healing rapidly. Or maybe it was the fresh mouse dinners. She was not sure which to credit, but it didn't matter much, as long as he was recovering. She had removed the bandage one day, as he had somehow loosened it and was dragging it around, and now he would flap his wings furiously while attempting to take off. But he would soon give up, as if he weren't ready, and would instead resort to strutting and preening himself. He always looked so dignified.

She had become quite attached to Harris and he had become dependent on her, an arrangement they both seemed to like for the time being. He would now even let her stroke his smooth, feathered head, but she had the utmost respect for him and always approached cautiously. He was still a wild and unpredictable bird and she knew that someday he would flap his wings and be gone, back to where he belonged. But for now, he was her company — actually her best friend and confidant. She could share anything with Harris. She truly dreaded the day when he would leave, but understood that it was destined to be.

She blew him a kiss and went out into the sun-filled

day. It was one of those days a person couldn't help but smile at — summer at its peak. Her body felt good, her mind felt clearer, her spirit had purpose, and she shined.

Arriving in town, she found a pay phone and called Ginger. She mentioned that she had overheard a woman at the lodge talking about a vision quest, and that she was interested in finding out more information about it. Ginger was pleased that she had called and gave her the number of a local medicine man who conducted such quests. Ginger also invited her to the next Moon Lodge ceremony. She was surprised that a month had gone by already.

She dialed the number that Ginger gave her, but received no answer, so she decided to roam about the town a little to waste time. She had never really investigated the small town thoroughly. She went into a small cafe to have a cup of tea while she waited. The place was busy, so she sat at the counter, which was the only empty place. Summer was the busiest time in this tourist town, but in a few months many of the stores would close down and things would get very quiet.

She ordered an herbal tea with lemon, and glanced around the old building. It was quaint and she had the feeling it was family owned. The man sitting to her left was reading the newspaper want ads and, while reaching for his drink, he didn't pay attention and knocked it over. All over her! Her pants were soaked. The man scrambled to get some napkins and began soaking up the spilled mess, patting her leg to try to dry her jeans. She looked over at him, embarrassed, but laughing. He seemed very flustered, but nothing could ruin her mood today.

He was a neatly dressed, tall man, and had a strange coloring. She couldn't decide whether he was American Indian or not. She knew from Grandfather's talks that many Indians lived near town.

As he repeatedly apologized, she caught a glimpse of his eyes. They were blue, deep blue, ocean blue, and were incredibly familiar. They offset his dark skin and almost glowed. No, she decided, he surely can't be Native American with those eyes.

She introduced herself and waved off his apologies, claiming she was okay and straightening her clothes. He asked her if she was just visiting town, as he had not seen her before, and she explained that she was staying at her grandfather's cabin just outside town in Bluebird Canyon. Yes, he nodded his head, that is a beautiful place.

Suddenly, he glanced over to her, incredible blue eyes piercing through her. She felt as if she were being undressed and unconsciously blushed. Their eyes met and a chill went through her. She felt like she was in another world, or like he was from one. Taking a deep breath, she raised her eyebrows in question, and he looked away as suddenly as he had started.

He reached around his neck and undid one of the many necklaces hanging there. He crumpled it in his hand, looked up to the ceiling, and mumbled a quick prayer that she strained to hear. Holding out his large, dark hand, he offered her the necklace. Still entranced by his look, she accepted it silently, a surprised expression on her face.

He spoke deeply and clearly, words she would never forget, "This gift I share with you. I can see your distress, your sickness, but I can also see your light. You are on the right path and your desire to be healed is close at hand. Please accept this gift of my ancestors. It will give your spirit strength and your heart guidance. Wear it in peace. Ho!"

With a nod of his head, he gathered up his newspaper, placed his right hand on her shoulder, looked deep into her eyes and smiled, then slowly walked out the door, long braided hair swinging gently with his gait.

She sat there with her mouth open for at least five minutes. Trancelike, his words echoed in her head, and she gripped the necklace tightly. She felt exhilarated and realized that, in her amazement, she had not even looked at the necklace or said thank you. Holding onto the warm memory, she cast her glance downward and examined her gift. It was a short necklace with alternating silver and wood beads, an emblem hanging from the bottom. The emblem was a hand-carved wooden circle with a large bird in the center, maybe a hawk or an eagle. She was not sure. A cross divided the circle and the bird into four sections. She wondered what it symbolized. It was very nicely done, full of detail and well worn. Clutching the necklace, she realized from the man's words that he must be of American Indian descent, and she felt honored.

She finished her tea and began to wonder if what had just happened was a dream, because it had felt like one. She paid her tab and asked the waitress if she was familiar with the man who had sat next to her. The waitress said he had been coming in for years. His family lived to the west of town and their name was Dark Horse. His name was Reno Dark Horse.

She thanked the lady and, with a bounce in her step, she was out the door. Life was so full of surprises, she thought. Excited, she returned to the pay phone to make her call, but still no one was home, so she drove back to Bluebird Canyon.

Chapter Nine

 She and Harris spent many quiet days together enjoying the summer sun and the forever-blue skies. The cabin had become their sanctuary, and thoughts of healing and peace were evident everywhere. Crookedly stacked books covered the tables, filled with different ideas on health issues, American Indian lore, dreams, and metaphysical ramblings. Her desire to understand things to which she had never before given credence overwhelmed her. She absorbed page after page of writings, never tiring, and the thoughts and ideas filled her head and gave her strength.

She learned about energy and auras, reincarnation, dream weaving, American Indian philosophies and rituals (which were now of interest to her because of her meeting with Reno Dark Horse), crystals, acupuncture, massage, color healing and a variety other seemingly endless ideas. There was an incredible amount of information available, but she took it in at a relaxed pace and utilized every bit to her advantage by trying to put it into perspective in her life. Inspired, she chose subjects that felt right to her. Some of the ideas seemed totally bizarre, while others fit right into the issues that life now held before her. Dreaming, positive thinking, and psychic energy were the topics that gained most of her attention. Her years of confusion melted away in the transparent nature of truth. One book she read stated:

"Anything you dream has possibility. If your mind can think something, it can happen. The power of a thought is the most underestimated event in life. Focusing on one thought over and over can bring unrivaled results, especially in the case of health. Your mind controls your body, controls your every cell, and if your mind can tell those cells to be happy, to reproduce normally, they obey and change. The key is positive thinking. Positive thinking creates a healthy, vital energy flow that keeps the body functioning normally. Negative thinking results in blocked energy patterns and creates havoc in the organs, especially the heart. We have an amazing power available to us. Let us take advantage of our superior intelligence and harmonize our minds with others who are thinking positively and our strength will be tenfold. Why suffer when you can live fully, with excitement at being alive and healthy! Choose life!"

Skipping a few pages, she continued reading:

"Dreaming delights all. When you dream, the life force is projecting ideas and reality. Take advantage of this power by recognizing the potential and drawing it into your life. Use your dreams to enhance the daily episodes you encounter. If you recognize the subtle signs, the dreams can direct your path, as there are many roads to take and it is easy to be confused. You must read the symbols and interpret their meaning in your mind. No one can do this for you. Only you can make sense of them, as the symbols are written in a language you have subconsciously created and only you can decipher the information. Pay attention and look within honestly. Good dreams and bad dreams can both be used for positive results if you pay attention to their meaning. It is a message from above. Live it!"

▶ ◀

It felt as if the author had written these passages just for her. The information was astounding in that it addressed her heartfelt thoughts. It opened a whole new avenue to her healing approach. It gave validity to the feelings she had always had. She knew inside that her mind had power over her body. It made perfect sense. There had to be some intelligence that controlled all functions of the body — breathing, pumping blood, healing cuts — and if the mind could organize those great feats, it surely could reverse the cancer. She felt she had been ignorant for so long. They had never taught her this stuff in school.

So many ideas were floating around in her head that she felt she had to organize them into some tangible form so she could apply them to her daily life. She began to think of all the experiences she had had that impressed her and wrote them down.

She began at the beginning. She had been an only child, overprotected and doted on every day. Money had never been a problem in her family, and her parents had hired a nurse to care for her. She had had everything she needed, physically that was, but there had been some part of her that had never felt quite fulfilled. She had never sensed as if anyone really understood her, and had not known quite where to turn with her problems. Even a young child has problems that need to be addressed by a loving and comforting parent. It had been as if she were not supposed to have any problems, as if the material fufillment would take care of everything. She could remember her parents praising her: "She's such a good little girl." It echoed in her head. She had never felt good, except of course with Grandfather. He had always listened. But when she had tried to tell her parents any of this, they had responded by assuring her that nothing was wrong and that she would grow out of it. So, consequently, she had begun to think that she had no real problems. She had just tried to live up to the 'good girl' image. She had soon become very good at projecting this image, and the turmoil of her years had been stuffed down inside, hidden beneath her facade. It had served her situation to show her well-meaning parents that she was fine and that, of course, they were right again.

Grandfather had been the black sheep of the family, the thinker. He was the one who had made all the money, but he was considered a unique and unorthodox old man. She had been his favorite, and during their much too rare gatherings, she had spent a lot of time talking with him about things no one else seemed to care about. Grandfather had always had a knack for saying the right thing and making her feel normal again. She had lived for the days they spent together.

That was probably why she had chosen the cabin for her dying retreat. It was of Grandfather's making, and to her, every log and board held his hopes and dreams. Its aura was calm and soothing to her. It was as if he were still in the house with her, giving her strength and inspiration, and guiding her along. That one thought alone was so comforting.

The rest of her life she considered fairly normal, except for one event that she still hadn't come to terms with. Grandfather had died when she was 24, just as she was finishing college. It had been difficult, but she had been prepared for it as he had been ill for many years. There had been nothing left unsaid between them, and it had seemed that his death had finalized a stage in her life, for soon afterwards she had met the man of her dreams. He had been similar to Grandfather in many respects, mostly in his accepting nature, a trait she had come to appreciate, and she had just shifted her loyalty and trust from one man to the other. They had planned to marry, but one month before the wedding was to have taken place, her fiance had died in a plane crash. It had been almost one year to the day after Grandfather's death. It had been sudden, and it had torn her apart. She had never been the same after that day. Having nowhere to place her trust, no one who truly believed in the real her, she had begun again, as she had learned early on, to deny her true feelings and to forge beyond them, with a heart like an icicle.

She had lived this kind of glacial existence until she had gotten sick. She had almost been glad. Death could then be seen as a comfort, a way out of having to deal with the pain. The once precious child could then return to the light from whence it had come.

How can anyone deal with the image that they are not known for who they really are? That they have sacrificed their own being for the satisfaction of others? To be so untrue is perjury to the soul. Totally unforgivable. Do we need to be accepted by others at such a cost that we will deny our own destinies to please others? Yes. It is a sad but truthful fact of reality.

She had certainly hoped to die before she got this far, but the revealing personality of death leaves no stone unturned. Now that her quest had unknowingly turned towards life, the pain had surfaced. Either way, she had to deal with it face to face. Her desire to share her discoveries with others lit the fire on the candle in her heart, and the iceberg began to melt. She began to feel again, to become curious about life, to explore the yet uncharted regions of her soul. It was incredible.

Every day was so new and exciting. It was as if she had been given one last chance to figure things out. She began to feel blessed that she had been inflicted with cancer. It had become the pivot point for enhancing her life, and without it she would still be in the city, shuffling back and forth to her job, ignoring the beauty around her, ignoring the pain in her heart, silently crying.

She knew it was only a beginning and that there were more dilemmas to face, but if she could endure the unfathomable anguish of the past, then everything else could be handled with grace.

Chapter Ten

She prepared to go meet the medicine man. Finally having gotten her call through, she had talked to the man's wife and gotten directions. She still did not know his name or what to expect.

She sat down to meditate and organize her thoughts before she left, as she wanted to be clear about her goals and intentions. Inhaling deeply, she centered herself and grounded her body to the Earth with a visualization of a thick rope extending from her spine into the Earth. She had read about this exercise in her studies and found that it aroused stability — that even the process of concentrating on the visualization helped to focus her thoughts. Meditation intrigued her. She realized that the goal was to be there, yet not there — to clear one's mind. While she had no trouble clearing her mind, she couldn't fathom the idea of not being where she was. Maybe it took time.

Ten minutes passed and Harris became very curious. He approached cautiously, meandering closer and closer until he was right by her side. Tilting his head, curious owl eyes bright, he wondered why she was so still. Feeling a presence, she opened her eyes to see Harris standing directly in front of her, and their eyes met in a long and deep stare. His gaze was intense and unyielding. She sensed an incredible strength and wisdom in him, an energy that sent shivers down her back. If he could only talk, she thought longingly, what wonders he would have to tell.

Instinctively she perceived that the timing was right and, reaching over to the woodstove, she grabbed a pair of old leather gloves. Recalling her owl learnings, she pressed her index finger against the back of his legs, just above the feet. Most birds will more easily walk forward onto a hand, but owls prefer to step backwards. To her amazement, Harris did not resist. He sensed her calm and love for him, and finally felt safe with her. She realized that they had communicated far beyond what any words could have said and, giving him a gentle hug, she planted a kiss on top of his head.

"So, you want to come with me, big guy?" she questioned affectionately. Harris just sat there, bird feet gripping her fingers tightly. She decided that one squeeze meant yes and two squeezes meant no. Harris just squeezed once.

Harris traveled well in the car although the ride was nearly an hour. It was late morning when they arrived and truly a beautiful summer day, without a cloud in the sky. She went up to the front door of an old, large house. It was a two-story wooden house, recently painted a dark brick red, and around the side she could see where they had attached an adobe addition which housed a small greenhouse. They were in the process of building a large deck on the front of the house, and that was where she stood now, hoping that someone had heard her knock.

Finally she was greeted by a woman, a beautiful olive-skinned lady who seemed somehow ageless except for the gray streaks in her long braided hair. The woman introduced herself as Sheila, Hank's wife, and pointed to a small group of men working in a field behind the house. She felt at ease with Sheila, and wanted to talk with her longer, but the phone rang inside the house, so she thanked her quickly and stepped down from the deck.

Approaching the group of men, she felt nervous butterflies in her stomach. She took a deep breath and summoned up some courage, and when she was within calling distance, she yelled, "Hello!"

One man walked to her, and shook her hand excitedly. He was shorter than her, with a somewhat shriveled look, and she tried to imagine what he had looked like when he had filled up his skin. His copper eyes glowed and his full head of shortly cut hair glistened in the sun. He had a fiery enthusiasm and she immediately liked him.

"I've come to talk with someone about a vision quest," she explained.

"Yes, yes. I understand. Glad to meet you. My name is Hank Dark Horse and these are my sons, Reno and Steve," he replied as he pointed behind himself.

It was him! Surprised, she clutched the necklace around her neck. Both men turned to wave at her and her eyes locked with Reno's, a wave of recognition shooting between them. He smiled and nodded his head; she gave an embarrassed little wave and her heart fluttered.

"Ah, so I see you two have met," Hank said as he inspected the necklace she was gripping. She nodded shyly, but before she could explain, Hank led her to a circle of wooden benches and sat down. "Come and sit," he said, "let's talk."

She began, telling him her story from the beginning, emphasizing her recent studies and experiences. She explained how Ginger had given her his number. She expressed how much she had learned from nature and how she felt a true union with all life, and how she had learned a lot from Harris, her owl, but that she needed direction and guidance and hoped that a vision quest would help.

"You have an owl?" Hank asked unbelievably. Up until now, Hank had been sitting quietly and listening intently, but this was something he had to know more about.

"Oh, yes I do," she replied, "Just a minute and I'll introduce you."

She ran down the driveway and opened the car door to find Harris sleeping peacefully in the warmth. "Sorry about leaving you so long," she cooed to the sleepy bird, glad that she had left a window open. She put on her gloves and gently picked him up, stroking his wings to reassure him.

Harris was very shy around this new person and recoiled when Hank tried to touch him. She could feel Harris begin to panic, his talons gripping her finger tightly, so she explained to Hank about Harris's dislike for being handled. She said that since she had spent so much time with him, they had become friends and now he trusted her.

Hank was impressed with their relationship and had a lot of questions to ask. "An owl is a very sacred bird, and I can see that the spirits have brought him to you," he said, staring at the woman and her bird. They were an unusual pair and he was surprised that the owl had endured the accident. He decided that he would help her.

"Let us talk now about the reason you are here — the vision quest," directed Hank. "The vision quest is a long and trying experience, but it brings much wisdom and healing of the spirit. It is a four-day-long ritual. First we must have a sweat lodge ceremony for purification and prayer, and then I will take you to a sacred spot on the mountain," he pointed to the south, "where you will sit and pray for four days and nights. You must fast, with no food or water, and you shall be wrapped in a blanket for warmth. Hopefully you will receive visions and knowledge through your sacrifice. I will come and check on you once a day to make sure you are okay. A woman as sick as you are needs to be very careful. Then, when the fourth day is over, I will bring you down from the mountain and we will have another sweat lodge ceremony. Then we can discuss your experience. Do you think you can do all this?" Hank finished.

She pondered the question slowly, to be sure she understood it all and was making the right decision. Listening to Hank made the vision quest sound more serious and difficult than she had imagined. It would take a lot of effort on her part. She shuddered as she thought of being out in the woods all night by herself. Sleeping outside on Grandfather's porch was a different story.

"Are there wolves or coyotes or other dangerous animals in these woods, like bears?" she asked, feeling pale.

"Yes, there are a few foxes and coyotes, but there are more elk, deer, and rabbits than anything else. Do not fear the four-legged ones. They are your friends and will not harm you. The medicine will watch over you and guide you," Hank reassured her.

"The medicine?" she questioned.

"The spirits that assist me will be with you on the mountain," Hank said, "giving you visions. They will use their powers to keep you from harm."

She looked at this man with admiration. She had already gained a deep respect for his centeredness, his certainty. He seemed so calm and peaceful, so sure of what he said. She had only one question left.

"May I bring Harris with me?" she asked, eyes full of hope.

"Of course," Hank replied, "I think Harris will be good company for you and he may even get some healing help himself!" They laughed together as Harris cocked his head to one side and issued a high squeal.

"Looks like he agrees with us!" chuckled Hank, as he turned to see his son, Reno, approaching.

"Sounds like you two are getting along quite well," said Reno. Seeing the owl, he exclaimed, "Oh, so that's what all the excitement is about." Reno kneeled down in front of her to get a better look at the bird, and Harris coiled back into her arms. She was pleased that Harris trusted her.

"Shy little fellow. Does he have a name?" Reno asked as he reached out to stroke the bird.

"His name is Harris," she replied, "and he is going on my vision quest with me." She smiled at Hank.

Reno looked up at her with surprised amusement, trying to picture the two of them perched atop the mountain. He looked into her eyes — eyes that seemed full of hope, yet radiated much sadness. He felt a pain in his heart for this young woman, as well as a certain familiarity. He wanted to reach out and hold her to ease the suffering, just as he had wanted to that day in the cafe. The memory of her had haunted him for a week. He looked away quickly, a little embarrassed, then cleared his throat and said with a smile, "So when do you climb the mountain?"

She looked towards Hank, questioning with her eyes. Hank thought for a moment and said, "There are a few things that we need to do to prepare you for the quest, but I think next week will work out well for me, unless of course, you need more time."

"No," she explained, "I would rather not have too much time to prepare for it. I might change my mind." She laughed.

"Well, then," said Hank, "Sunday is the new moon and would be a good day to begin. Does that sound all right to you?"

She nodded her head in agreement and Hank turned to his son. "Reno, I would like you to assist me with this. Do you think you can make it?"

"Yes, I think I can fit it into my busy schedule," he joked. Then, turning to her, he said, "I feel this vision quest will be a very healing time for you. Do you still have the necklace?"

She nodded, reaching into her blouse to expose it. "Do you want it back?" she questioned.

Reno smiled, his pearly whites shining, "No," he said, "it is yours to keep, but I think it would be a good idea for you to bring it with you to the mountain. It will give you power and protect you."

She grasped the necklace tightly, a glimmer of fear in her eyes, wondering what she needed to be protected from.

Again, Reno smiled, saying, "The mountain is friendly. Don't worry. One of us will be up every day to check on you."

They smiled at each other and felt as if they had known each other before. There was a familiar feeling in their friendship, and she felt safe and reassured.

Hank watched the two of them, wondering about the necklace and their obvious attraction. An interesting woman, he thought, as he stood up to finish the meeting. He had a lot of work to do.

"I think it would be a good idea for you to buy a pipe to accompany you on this journey. There are also many preparations we need to do for the lodge. Pouches must be tied, sage and stones gathered, and wood cut. Why don't you return the day before the ceremony to assist me?" inquired Hank. He then explained to her where to buy a pipe and what she needed to do with it. Lastly he warned her, "Please stay away from all drugs and alcohol. Your mind should be clear and open, ready for inspiration."

She assured him that she would be prepared and thanked him for all his help. What a blessing it was to find such wonderful people! She left their ranch with a warm, tingly feeling, excited about the future and the quest.

"Well, Harris," she whispered into the bird's ear, "we are finally going to do it. I feel as if my life has just begun."

Chapter Eleven

 The week before the vision quest was like a dream. The days blurred into each other as only one thought permeated her mind: how to share her new-found revelations with the world. It was difficult to think about how to convey something that had taken her so long to realize — how to put it in some form that would make it interesting to others. She began to doubt herself. Were the ideas that she had come to terms with unimportant to others? How many people were really willing to look deeply and honestly within their hearts, to make their souls transparent? She decided that there had to be at least a few, and if it made as much of a difference to one other person's struggle between life and death as it had made to her own, then it would all be worth it. She hoped the vision quest would answer all her questions.

She prepared the best she could, and tried to eat less food to shrink her stomach a bit. Her appetite wasn't great, but she tended to get dizzy if she waited long periods between meals. She made an effort, as well, to eat all the perishable food she had on hand so that it would not spoil while she was gone. Her refrigerator was mostly filled with vegetables, fruit, cheese, and milk, so what she could not eat she would just leave out for the birds and chipmunks. She was beginning to enjoy her vegetarian diet, and did not miss the meat at all. She had even stopped eating eggs, which she had never really liked, and knew that someday she would stop using all animal products, including butter and cheese. But her system was fragile, and she took the dietary changes one step at a time, not wanting to force an intense cleansing until she felt strong enough. Her new diet left her feeling light and clear, and despite her illness she felt more energetic. The only meat now left in the house was Harris' reserve of frozen beef hearts, and he would probably polish those off before they left.

She was excited, but anxious, as she thought of the four nights she would have to spend outside. It was the ultimate test of strength and courage for her, a total abandonment of all the securities of life, an offering of herself in complete trust to the universe. She shuddered at the thought of being so vulnerable.

I don't have to do this, she thought, relieved. It's like some primitive legend that has exaggerated the truth. It has absolutely no scientific bearing and I am probably just wasting my time.

She sighed. She had no other choice. She could not go back to chemotherapy. This was the path she had chosen, which she hoped was the path to her health, and she had never expected it to be easy.

She was not afraid of dying — death was her close friend. She was not afraid of being alone — she lived that way every day. She probed her mind to discover what she was really afraid of. The answer came quickly, and although it was hard to acknowledge, it had surfaced from her heart.

I am afraid of becoming well, she thought. I am afraid

that I will have to return to my old lifestyle, that I will have to participate in the 'real' world again.

The past offered her little hope. She had begun to almost enjoy her disease. It had given her an excuse to be reckless, to be irresponsible and selfish. But most of all, it had allowed her to be free. Deep inside she liked it. This was a great realization for her, a big step in understanding the process. Subconsciously she had created this illness because she was unhappy with her life. Her losses had been too great. She had become an emotional refrigerator, numb to any sensations of joy. The disease had grown on the discontent soil of her heart. It had come as a deadly warning: "This is not how life was meant to be. You must change or die."

She sat perfectly still, eyes glazed, staring distantly at nothing, acutely aware of her mistakes at that moment. She felt like a child again, and wished someone would hold her and understand her pain. She had never realized it was so important to honestly feel every moment of life, to engage fully in the process of living.

She began to cry. Releasing the pain and resentment, she let go with long, shuddering sobs that tore at her heart. Her stomach, tense and tied in knots for so long, now yielded to the flow. She held back nothing. Her once-suppressed feelings poured out of her like water through the crumbling dam of a mighty river. The consuming current washed clean her diseased heart, and soon gentle waves lapped at the shorelines of her soul. This was the true beginning of her healing.

After this, things were more clear in her mind than they

had been in many years. Gathering up a pen and paper, she began to write, trying to express her innermost emotions:

> O that hearts may feel some joy
> Ancient love it drifts ashore
> Found by those wayward and lost
> A gift of hope for something more.
>
> The sorrow that one's heart endures
> Is masked beneath a life of steel
> Unyielding, cold and stagnant ways
> I must, once again, relearn to feel
>
> And in my dreams for unity
> For peace that reigns in all
> I find that love it echoes clear
> If I could but hear its call.

Writing seemed to lighten her heart, and she dried her tears. She felt chilled and tired, and although the sun had not yet set, she fed Harris, blew him a kiss, and lay down, falling instantly asleep. A vibrant, blue glow of peace surrounded her and her own deep, muffled breathing followed her into dreamland.

► ◄

She awoke to a knock on the door and voices calling her name. She arose quickly, put on her robe, and shuffled over to open the door. A few pairs of arms reached out to hold her, and before she knew it her house was filled with people.

"Mother, what are you doing here?" she asked, confused.

"Hello, dear. We missed you so much and were concerned, so we decided to come and visit you. There is no phone and well, you know, we were worried that you may not be doing all right, so Dad and I brought Grandma up to enjoy a day in the mountains," her mother declared as she walked around the house inquisitively, examining everything. "Are you feeling okay, honey? You don't look very good."

"Yes, Mother, I feel fine. I just woke up. I had no time to prepare for your visit." She ruffled her messy hair and rubbed the swollen bags under her eyes, the remnants of last night's tears. She silently wished that they would not be staying too long. She enjoyed her space and privacy, and hoped that they would not ask too many questions, as she was not at all prepared to answer them. She decided that they must have come because they somehow felt threatened by her release last night. She had mentally cut off all painful memories, and they were part of those memories.

A loud shriek brought her out of her thoughts. Her mother had found Harris. She was not sure which one of them looked more frightened — her mother or Harris — as she put on her gloves and reached down to pick up the shivering owl. "What in the world is that creature doing in here?" asked her mother, shocked but trying to regain her composure.

"It's just Harris, Mother, and he's an owl that lives with me. Now please settle down or you'll scare him. He's very sensitive," she informed her and proceeded to give a short account of how she and Harris had met.

Her mother looked a little pale thinking of an owl living in the house. Her father, who had been silent up until now, tried to comfort everyone by suggesting that they all go outside. It was a good idea for all involved, so she put Harris in her room, calming him with gentle words before closing the door.

They spent the morning talking about her health, the changes in their lives, Grandma's arthritis, gossip about relatives, and the weather. The final question, which she thought she had evaded, was finally asked. Her father had the honors.

"So dear, when are you coming home?" he asked hopefully. Her father, overweight and always serious, was the one who felt most responsible for her sickness. He felt that he had done something wrong, and that it was somehow his fault, but he had no idea what it could be. In his mind, she had never grown up, and he could not stand the thought of his little girl dying before he did.

She replied stubbornly, "This is my home now, father. I am not returning to the city. I have found peace here, and I think this is where my healing is. But if it is not, I'd rather die here amidst the beauty of nature than anywhere else. At least my final days will be happy ones." She wanted to be clear and to the point so that there would be no misunderstanding.

Her parents looked at each other questioningly and her mother responded, "But it is almost winter, and there is no heat in the house. How will you survive? How will you plow the driveway? What if there is an emergency?" Her mother was the pessimist of the family. She had always had the desire to inform everyone else of the worst possibilities that could occur.

Patiently, she replied, "I will cut trees and burn them in the stove. There is plenty of wood around here. Isn't that how you and Grandfather spent the winters here, Grandma?"

"Yes my dear, that's right. But your dear Grandfather, bless his heart, was a young man then, and he did all the work of hauling and splitting the wood. A sick girl like yourself should not be working so hard. It is dangerous. Listen to your mother, please," her Grandma pleaded.

The city is dangerous as well, she thought. "Please don't worry about me. I am sure I can manage. I appreciate your concern, but I have made a few friends. I will get help from someone if I have any trouble," she assured them.

The three of them shook their heads in disbelief, unaware of her newly declared ambitions and strength. They were sure a winter in the mountains would weaken her, but they had no choice but to accept her decision. She was a grown woman and had made up her mind — rather willfully, they thought.

"Well, then, will you join us for lunch?" asked her father. "We're going to Grandma's favorite spot in town and then we must be on our way home. We want to be out of the mountains before it gets dark."

"I'd love to," she replied, "Give me a moment to clean up and get dressed."

They do care for me, and I know they are just trying to help, she thought as she headed for the bathroom, but can I be related to these people who are afraid to be up in the mountains at night? She chuckled silently. There is more danger at night in the city than there is anywhere up here. That's where I must get my reservations about the vision quest. She wondered if fear was genetic.

Knowing that her fear of the dark was based on her prior existence seemed to dispel it. What would they say if they knew about her plans to sit naked on a mountain for four days and nights without any food or water? They would think she was crazy. Plum out of her mind. They would probably commit her. She wished she could share with them all her new thoughts and ideas, and how she had grown in so many ways, but she knew they would not understand. Some day she would share it with them, if she lived to tell the story.

She entered her room to get dressed and gazed over at Harris, who was sitting on her bed where she had left him earlier. He hadn't moved. He seemed to be shaking his head in disbelief, and he looked at her as if to say, "Who are these people?"

"Don't worry, Harris, they will be leaving soon," she told him, "they must be from another planet."

Chapter Twelve

Yawning, she stretched her arms, awakening to another day and feeling stronger and happier than she had in weeks. Habitually locating the lymph nodes on the side of her neck, she noticed that they felt less swollen. A good sign, she thought happily. Tomorrow was the beginning of her vision quest and she wanted to be in the best of shape. The week had passed quickly.

She arose and searched the cabin for Harris, finding him huddled in a corner of the box-nest she had made for him. She had brought in a few fresh blades of grass and twigs from outside and it seemed like home to him — well, almost. She sat down by him and cooed some sweet sounds of affection as he blinked his sleepy eyes and stood perfectly still. The bandage had fallen off weeks ago and he still hadn't succeeded in flying, other than flapping his wings hopefully, going nowhere. She was worried that he had become too dependent on her for food and shelter, and that when he healed he would not want to leave. She just had to trust the workings of nature.

It would be a sad day when he did leave, she thought to herself. Then it occurred to her that he might never fly again, that the damage was irreversible. She knew inside her heart, though, that he would soon be gone. She was not sure how to prepare herself for the loneliness that Harris would leave behind. Stroking his feathered wing, she told herself that it was for the best. I love you, she mouthed silently to the owl, and stood up to begin preparing for the day.

Anticipating the warmth of the sunlight, she hurried outside, a glass of juice in one hand and a note pad in the other. She needed to write a list for the day. First on her agenda was to buy a prayer pipe. Hank had told her where to look for one in town. She was not exactly sure what she was looking for, but at the Moon Lodge ceremony last night one of the women had showed her the pipe she used. It was a beautiful pipe, with a lot of detailed beadwork. It looked as if it had taken days to assemble.

She had attended the Moon Lodge ceremony still high in spirits. A few of the women had been familiar, and others she had never seen before. It had rained earlier in the day and the damp, cool earth had felt good to be on. They had sung a chant that still echoed in her head this morning:

WAY A HEY NE YO, WAY A HEY NE YO
O WAY A HEY NE YO, O WAY A HEY NE YO
YO, A WAY HA YO, A WAY HA YO, A WAY HA YO
YO, A WAY HA YO, A WAY HA YO, A WAY HA YO

It was a song that brought the spirit down and balanced it with the Earth. A very centering chant, enjoyable to sing, it had set a good mood to begin the ceremony. Each Moon Lodge ceremony had focused on a theme so that all prayers could be united towards one objective. The theme for this lodge had been world peace/inner peace, which again seemed appropriate for her.

The woman who had opened the prayers had begun, "Welcome all to this sacred lodge of the sisters. We give thanks to the Creator and our guardians for bringing us together here on this day. May our prayers be in truth and our hearts open to receive inspiration and to heal our pain. Our strength and power is found in our thoughts and dedication to the purpose we have designated for ourselves. Be positive, live positive, and always offer a helping hand. We would like to focus this day on creating world peace. We believe this is only possible through inner peace. Focus your thoughts, still your mind, and think thoughts of peace and reconciliation. If all people did this just once a day, peace would abide on Earth. But we must begin with us. By raising the quality of our thoughts, we will inspire others to do the same without even saying a word. May we join together in hope for the good of all and pray for the great day. My sisters, my friends."

All had replied, "HO!"

Each woman had prayed in turn and sacred herbs had been burned on the hot coals. It had been very beautiful and uplifting, and they had all cried together at the disease of violence in this world. They had each also realized the power they had as individuals to deny and transform this disease. They had held hands tightly, a small but dedicated group, and had felt peace in each other's strength. Together they could make a difference.

She had left the lodge soothed and relaxed, her heart rejoicing in her new-found friends. She had the feeling that no matter where she was, she would never be alone. Their spirits were locked in purpose. She felt as if she had found some people who were from the same planet she was from.

At last, she sighed to herself, aliens, friendly aliens just like me.

Feeling warm and tingly after recalling the ceremony, she put her attention again on writing her list. It was hard to concentrate on such a lovely day, though. The tall ponderosa trees towered in the distance, and sunshine streamed down in brilliant rays through the pine needles. It was so beautiful, untouched by humanity. The chipmunks were darting in and out of an old fallen tree, gathering and playing, at one with their world. The emptiness was so full, the silence so relaxing. She breathed deeply, closed her eyes, and let the warm rays of the sun caress her face. Paradise.

▶ ◀

She gave up the list-writing idea and, as it was getting late in the morning, gathered up the things she needed and prepared to leave for town.

She arrived at the store, a trading post of sorts, feeling a bit awkward. She was not sure exactly what she wanted and did not know how to explain her needs to a salesperson. The store was filled with many beautiful things: woven blankets with bright colored patterns hanging on the walls, intricate beadwork, unusual looking clothing, feathers of all kinds, and ancient looking artifacts. It was as if she had entered another century. She enjoyed wandering around.

She finally stumbled upon a shelf of pipes, all large and sacred looking, but she was afraid to touch any of them. A saleslady approached her and they discussed what she needed. This wasn't as difficult as she had anticipated.

The woman opened a locked case and showed her a variety of pipes, their prices ranging widely. The long, wooden stems all seemed to be carved by hand, having a narrow, hollow center, a mouthpiece at one end, and a short, carved extension that fit snugly into the pipe bowl at the other end. The bowls looked hand-carved as well, and were made of a soft, red rock which the saleslady informed her was pipestone. Some of the carvings were exquisite and very detailed, while others were more simple and plain.

She looked at each one as the saleslady patiently waited. She did not want to spend a lot of money and chose one with gentle, simple lines, which was fine with her. On her way to the cashier, however, her eye caught a pipe in one of the display cases. It was a deep red color, and at the front of the bowl was a bird, its wings extended to either side. She asked to have a look at it, and fell in love with it right away. It was probably supposed to be an eagle, but it reminded her of Harris trying to fly, and she thought the resemblance was remarkable. The back of the bird was the bowl itself and the carver had intricately detailed the feathered wings. She felt that it was a very creative work of art, tastefully done.

She glanced at the bottom, looking for the price, and when she saw it her mouth dropped open in shock. She had that much money, because her father had insisted that she take his check the day he visited — probably out of guilt — but she hadn't really intended on spending that much. The saleslady was aware of her distress and, since that particular pipe had been in the store for quite a while, she offered the pipe to her at a ten-percent discount. It helped only a little, but she knew she had to have the pipe anyway, so she thanked the lady and purchased it excitedly.

When she arrived home, she showed it to Harris. "You are my mascot," she informed him with a smile. She then wrapped the pipe in some sage that Hank had given her and covered it with a piece of red cloth. Hank had been very explicit in his directions. She sat quietly with it for a moment, eyes closed humbly, hands carefully balancing this object that she assumed was holy, and said a quick prayer for health and strength. Then she gathered up her purse and a warm coat, picked up Harris, and drove to the Dark Horse house.

She had come, as they had decided, the day before she would begin the quest, to make the preparations that were necessary. With a nervous quiver in her stomach, she wondered if Reno would be there. She arrived in the early afternoon, and found that they had already begun. Hank and Reno were out back sawing dead wood into large pieces for the firepit that would heat the rocks for the sweat lodge ceremony.

"Good afternoon," she called, and they waved, motioning her to wait a minute for them as they were almost finished.

With Harris on one arm and the pipe in the other, she wandered around the ranch. It was in a beautiful setting, at the base of a large mountain, with many tall, leafy trees and a small creek that ran behind the house. There were piles of stuff everywhere: two-by-fours stacked near a large barn, heaps of metal rods, and a lot of other junk she couldn't identify. The sweat lodge was out back by the creek, but there were many other small outbuildings as well, scattered across the grounds. The area around the house was very nice: a cool-looking green lawn, newly mowed, with a run-down, rusty swing set and other chidren's toys strewn about. There was a large garage next to the house with four cars parked near it; two of them looked as if they hadn't been on the road in years. The place definitely had a lived-in look. These were hard working-folks and she felt comfortable here. There was no pretense, no expectation, no pressure; just a simple and honest existence. She had never known a home like this. It was just plain cozy.

Satisfied with her inspection, she returned to the woodcutting area where the men had just finished. "Great place you have here," she said enthusiastically.

Hank looked up and smiled. "It's been in my family for many generations and soon it will be my son's, to raise his children here," he said as he glanced over at Reno. "If he ever has any, that is."

Reno looked at his father, then at her, and the air seemed so thick that for a moment the thought remained between them, suspended. Reno wriggled his eyebrows at her mischievously and she blushed a deep red, looking to the ground to avoid his gaze.

Suddenly Reno and Hank burst out in laughter, amused with their own charade. She looked up, embarrassed, but the laughter was contagious, and she began to laugh as well, realizing that it had all been a joke. At her expense.

"You must excuse us for our humor," Hank told her apologetically. "We tend to get carried away."

"You're excused," she told them, smiling at Reno, and her blushed face began to pale.

"Hello, Harris," Reno said to the owl, and brushed the feathers on the top of the bird's head with his index finger. Surprisingly, the owl didn't resist. "You look like you are feeling better today," Reno continued, and she nodded in agreement.

"Let's look at what you have there," Hank said to her as she handed him the pipe that she had bought. He unrolled the red cloth, pleased that she had followed his directions well, and peered inside. He stared at it for what seemed like ages, his mouth dropped in astonishment.

She was afraid to question his obvious amazement, thinking maybe she had done something wrong. Hank showed it to Reno. They both looked at each other bewildered, and then set their gazes on her.

"Where did you buy this pipe?" inquired Reno, hungry for an answer.

Again, feeling embarrassed under their scrutiny, she replied nervously, "I bought it at the trading post in town. The store where Hank suggested I go. Why," she questioned, "is something wrong?"

Reno reached for the pipe, ignoring her queston, and held it up to the sky with great reverence, as if it were something precious.

Hank offered the solution. "Reno made this pipe after his first vision quest, but he had to sell it a few years back when we had no money. It is very special to him and you have done us a great honor by bringing it here. It is a good sign."

She took a deep breath, relieved that she had done something right. Reno looked at her, hard and deep, and nodded his thanks, a faint smile on his lips. Who was this woman, this magical, mysterious woman who had fallen suddenly into his life? he asked himself as he watched her standing there radiating relief, an owl perched on her hand.

She returned his glance, feeling the same as she had when he had given her the necklace in the cafe. She felt as if she had somehow repaid him.

"I will go buy another pipe," she told them, rising to leave, "so that Reno may keep his."

"NO!" Reno said powerfully. "I wish for you to use this pipe and keep it. It will give you great strength on your quest. It is the carving of one of my visions and holds the power of it. It is a joy for me to see it again. How can I thank you?"

"You already have," she said softly, revealing the necklace around her neck.

Their eyes met again and a gentle wave of love passed between them. She felt the chill of consequence, amazed at the unmistakable coincidence. She then told them the story of how she had chosen that particular pipe. They both listened silently and smiled when she was finished.

"Well, and now we have a lot of work to do, my friends, so let's get busy," Hank commanded as he walked over to the woodpile.

Reno handed her the pipe. "Let me show you the sweat lodge," he said. They walked off together towards the west.

Chapter Thirteen

Preparations kept her at the Dark Horse house for most of the day. The sweat was to be at tomorrow's dawn, so they planned to have everything ready the night before. She couldn't have imagined how much work was involved in preparing a sweat lodge ceremony.

After the wood was cut and piled next to the fire pit, they collected river rocks: smooth, round, large rocks that would be cooked in the fire pit until they were red hot. Someone would have to be up in the early morning hours to start the fire and have the rocks ready at dawn.

They tied pouches. This process was unfamiliar to her, as was most of the work, and it took her a while to coordinate her hands so that she could keep up with Reno. Tiny squares of fabric were filled with pinches of tobacco, then folded and tied at their centers along a string with each other. The squares were different colors: red, black, yellow, white, green, and blue. She was told that the colors represented the four directions, the Earth, and sky. When they were finished, the long, colorful string was rolled into a ball and set aside.

Reno explained to her that the American Indian spirits held tobacco sacred, and that these pouches were an offering to them for helping her through her vision journey. Again she felt a quiver of fear, wondering why she needed so much help and protection to do this quest. She tried to trust the process and, because of Hank and Reno's confidence and experience, she remained composed.

Hank and Sheila were working on another project. They were putting tobacco into colored cloth as well, but the cloth was in much larger pieces and each piece was tied separately. Hank explained that these were called flags, and they were another offering. He tied each one to a tall, painted stick.

It was getting late in the day and they had one more job to do. They had to collect sage. Reno signaled her to follow him and they walked down the road for about a half a mile until they came to a large meadow filled with a great array of plants: wildflowers, tall summer grasses, and other growing things that she considered to be weeds.

"Be careful of snakes," Reno told her, as he headed into the meadow.

"How in the world do I do that?" she replied, but he didn't hear her, so she just decided to walk slowly and carefully, remembering the snake in her dream.

She carefully observed the plant he was choosing; it was tall, blue-green, sweet smelling, and very abundant in this particular field. They filled a large plastic bag with the sage. When Reno thought that they had enough, he began to show her many other plants.

"What do you do with those weeds?" she asked him.

"Weeds?" he replied with a chuckle. "These weeds are herbs, sacred healing herbs that work better than most drugs. The Creator put these plants here to help us heal, and our work is to find which ones heal which illnesses. My family has been using these herbs for many years.

They are very powerful if harvested properly and used correctly."

"Yes, I have done a little research on herbs. I used comfrey to try to help Harris' wing to heal faster," she explained to Reno, "but out here in the field, they all look the same."

Reno continued to identify many of the plants, some with names she had heard of, and he described the healing effect of each one. She was very impressed with his knowledge, so she pointed out different ones and asked about them. Reno was not stumped once; he had a name and a use for every plant in the field.

She surveyed this unusual man, admiring his coppery brown skin, his tall, muscular physique, and the way the breeze ruffled his dusty, black hair. His clean-shaven face had a gentle, wide nose, thin, tight lips and eyes that were set widely apart. He stood straight and lean, and seemed so firmly rooted on the Earth that it was as if he were one of the plants he knew so much about. She watched his large, sinewy hands pick another herb and began to think about what it would feel like for those hands to hold her. She knew she would melt at his touch, lavishing in the affection and releasing the years of denial that had held her heart hostage. As her dreamy eyes were lost in this vision, Reno glanced up and caught the feeling of her mood. She flushed as he recognized her desire, but she could not look away as his eyes held her breathless. He reached out his hand to her, grasping her arm. Their closeness aroused an enchanting mood.

He spoke softly, "What are you thinking, blue-eyed one?"

She felt as if she were in a dream and began to sense a faintness in her body, swaying slightly in the stillness of the moment. She was extremely drawn to this man, yet it had been too long since she had let her attractions have free reign. She had also promised herself that she would not get involved in a relationship until she was well. She knew it would be harder to die if she loved a man deeply.

Caught off guard between her logic and her emotions, she sputtered out, destroying the mood, "Oh, uh, I was just wondering if you have an herb that will cure cancer."

His face broke out into a puzzled look and then, sensing her fear, he gently nodded and smiled a grin of understanding. Dropping her arm, he spoke clearly, arms gesturing to the field about him, "I am sure there is a plant that will help you, but you must find it. I do not know which one it is. Cancer is a very complicated disease, a puzzle you must put together yourself, for each person has a different reason for getting sick. If you find out why you chose this sickness then the rest will be easy. You must first unlock the mystery of your heart. We will guide you and show you the way, but you must do the work yourself. The answer is here."

He placed his hand on her heart and said, "Know yourself and then we can share each other with honesty." She quivered at his directness, the pressure of his hand on her chest. She felt a tear in the corner of her eye and, blinking to release it, squeezed his hand and nodded her agreement.

Quickly he turned, afraid to say any more, picked up the bag of sage, and walked back toward the road. Feeling adolescent and foolish, she wiped her tears and ran to catch up with this man who knew her so well, yet whom she had just met. She wished she hadn't reacted so strangely, especially when she thought she had herself figured out.

They walked back to the ranch without talking much, as they were both deep in thought. When they arrived it was dusk. She found Hank and inquired if there was more work that needed to be done, and he said he thought they were just about finished.

"Leave your pipe with me. I need to prepare it," Hank told her. "And go home and get some rest. You have a long journey ahead of you."

Thanking him, she said she would return an hour before sunrise. She walked to her car, tired but excited. Driving home slowly, she thought about Reno and what he had said to her. It had really hit home. She understood in her heart all the things he had told her, but she hadn't yet figured out how to live with integrity in her life. She knew it was an important step. It was time to grow up.

Chapter Fourteen

The night seemed to pass in an instant, and she awoke with the feeling that she hadn't slept at all. Rubbing her droopy eyes, she realized that her belly was quivering. Relax, she told herself, as she took a deep breath and yawned. She did some gentle stretches, feet extended over her head, toes touching the floor, trying to relieve her anxious condition.

The quest was a great challenge for her and she had to keep telling herself over and over that she could do it. Perhaps the anticipation would be the worst part. She tried to stop thinking about it. She focused her mind on the preparations at hand.

Gathering up the items that she had set aside the night before, she drank a large glass of water and contemplated that this would be the last drink she would have for quite a while. She savored it slowly, and with respect. Gently, she picked up Harris, who was wide awake, and went out into the still dark morning.

It seemed chilly for a summer's night, she thought as she gazed up into the moonless sky. The stars twinkled a friendly greeting. Up in the mountains a person could see so much more of the universe. The city lights tended to dull the stars' luster. The idea that so many lives, so many planets existed, made her feel non-essential. She wondered why she was trying to heal herself at all. Surely her life made no difference to the masses on Earth. Or to the beings in the sky, if there were any. I must have such a big ego, she decided, to think that one small person is relevant.

Then, realizing that she was late, she and Harris got into the car. She would have plenty of time to ponder this and other weighty questions on the mountain.

It was just beginning to get light as she pulled up to the Dark Horse house. She put on her gloves, coaxed Harris onto her fingers, and walked over to the fire, which was already blazing. They had begun to cook the rocks at 2:00 a.m., and the stones were now red hot. She didn't see anyone around, so she threw a few small pieces of wood on the fire, and backed towards the flames to warm herself.

"Good morning," a voice out of nowhere said, startling her. "Sunrise has always been my favorite time of day."

The fire lit up the face belonging to the voice. It was Reno.

"Yes, it is beautiful," she smiled, "but a bit chilly. Do you always get up before sunrise?"

"The darkness before the dawn is a very special time. The whole Earth is waking up, and each bird, tree, and animal is patiently awaiting the first rays of the sun. Everything is fresh and the spirits gather to rejoice the start of a new day. It is a wonderful time to pray and commune with your guardians," Reno explained to her as if he were reciting a play. He always seemed to know what to say and when to say it. Just like Grandfather. "But to answer your question, yes, most days I am up just before sunrise to prepare myself for the day," Reno concluded.

They were joined by Hank, who came crawling out of

the sweat lodge. "Ready for the big day?" he asked her as he gave her a fatherly hug.

"I guess so, just a little nervous," she told him as she gently and rhythmically stroked Harris.

"Well, good morning, Harris," Hank spoke to the bird. Reno threw some more wood on the fire. "Are you ready for the journey?" Hank asked jokingly. Harris didn't respond.

"Is there anything I can do to help this morning?" she asked.

"No, I think we're about ready, but the sweat will be much too hot for Harris, so you must find some place to leave him until we're finished," Hank told her.

She did not want to leave him outside as she feared that an animal might come around and frighten him, or that he might wander off, so she took him to her car. "You stay here, my friend, and I will come to get you when we are ready to go up on the mountain." She reassured him with a few strokes and Harris let her know he understood with a loud "hoot, hoot."

She returned to the fire. A couple of Hank's friends had arrived to join them in the sweat and she introduced herself. She counted seven people, and was glad that there were a lot of folks. She had always enjoyed the moon lodges when lots of women participated. More people seemed to give the ceremony more energy, more life.

The sky was bright when Hank announced that they were ready. They all stood in a line, facing east, and prepared to fill their pipes. She stood next to Hank and he handed her pipe to her, teaching her how to fill it with the tobacco and herb mixture. Hank began by praying to each direction, then to the Earth and the sky, and lastly to the Creator. His prayer was fluent and beautiful, full of words in some other language that she could not understand. It was obvious that he had done this many times before. She watched him with respect, amazed with the reverence with which he did everything in life. No wonder Reno seemed to know so much; he had a good teacher.

The group starting singing a chant, a beautiful song that felt good to listen to, but since it was in another language as well, probably an Indian tongue, she only had an idea as to what it meant. She made a mental note to ask Hank about it later. She listened carefully to the song and soon tried to join in. It made her happy to sing.

Hank then took from her the necklace Reno had given her and the pipe, and placed them on a simple earthen altar — a rock circle filled with pouches, pipes, and other sacred objects she couldn't identify.

They undressed modestly, leaving on only their underwear, hung their clothes on a tree branch, and wrapped themselves with towels. She followed Hank into the lodge, clockwise, with everyone else behind her except Steve and Reno, who stayed outside to shovel in the red hot rocks. She was chilled in the dawn air, but her eyes soon adjusted to the light and she inspected her surroundings. She was seated between Hank and his wife on a soft layer of sage, the very same sweet-smelling stuff that she had picked with Reno. Sheila showed her how to rub herself with the sage so her body would smell sweet. It made her feel earthy.

The lodge was constructed of many small trees, which she thought must be aspen. They had been bent over and stuck in the ground to compose a half-circular structure. The poles were wrapped with different colored cloth, creating a rainbow effect, and were then covered with tarps and blankets, forming a little hut that was not even big enough to stand up in. She decided that seven people was the limit on how many the lodge would hold.

A door was left open to the east, and through it Reno was dropping red rocks into a pit dug in the middle of the lodge. Surprised by the quantity of stones that Reno and Steve alternately shoveled in, she realized that she was very warm now, as the heat of the rocks took away the chill.

Finally, Reno and Steve joined them, completing the circle, and spread blankets over the door to block out all the light. This was very effective, for now it was pitch black and even warmer.

Hank poured some water on the rocks, producing a loud hissing sound, and she could sense the billows of steam rising to the roof and curling down to touch each body. Hank began chanting, again an unfamiliar song to her, but everyone else knew the words and joined in. She listened closely, trying to sing along, but the words were too strange and the rhythm kept changing. So she just relaxed and enjoyed the soothing sounds.

More water was poured on the rocks and the air began to get very hot, almost uncomfortable, so she let her towel slide down her back to the ground. Beads of perspiration formed on every part of her body and dripped to the earth. As the heat increased, she curled down to be close to the cool, damp, sage-covered bottom. She could not stretch out, because of the crowded conditions, so she was content to just try to breathe the coolest air.

Hank began to pray, a long and unusual prayer, again filled with strange sounds and words. She began to think he would never stop, and just when she thought she could take the heat no more, he told her it was her turn to pray.

Taking a deep breath of steamy air, she began, "Thank you, Great Spirit, brothers and sisters of this lodge, and my guardians, for bringing me here today. I am blessed and filled with honor at the journey that is before me. I hope that I can be worthy of this quest and that all your efforts will be rewarded tenfold. I can never thank you enough for all you have given me: strength, courage, and loving guidance. I am eternally indebted. I pray that my healing will be a part of the world's healing and that the power I hope to gain will be used for the benefit of all. I ask for protection and inspiration on this quest, and for visions of peace and beauty. My spirit sings a sweet song of love to all my family here, for you are truly my relatives. Oh, yes, and I would like to pray that Harris be healed and be able to fly once again. My friends."

A deep "HO" resounded all around the lodge, and she wiped her eyes to dry the tears that had fallen, but found that they had mingled with her sweat and that it didn't matter. Tears were sweat and sweat was tears.

The lodge door was opened and a cool breeze entered the room, refreshing everybody. They all breathed deeply of the fresh air. Hank passed around a cup full of cold water for each person to drink or pour on themselves, whichever they needed. She slurped her portion down, as she knew she would need the moisture. Before they had cooled down completely, the door was closed again, and more water was poured on the rocks.

After they had sung another chant, the prayers began with the person to her left, Sheila. The heat seemed twice as hot as before, if that was possible, and it stung her skin. She crouched close to the ground and rocked herself to a silent tune as she listened. Sheila's prayer was beautiful, and she could tell by the words that Sheila was a very humble person. The prayer circled the room, and Sheila's words began to harmonize with the music in her mind, creating a song of love and serenity that lulled her thoughts to peace.

Her nostrils seemed on fire, and she could feel waves of heat, as if a large bird were flying around inside the lodge, its giant wings moving the air. She looked up to see if anything was there, but it was so dark that all she could see were brilliant flashes of blue light all around the lodge. She could not sense any boundaries and thought for a moment that she was gazing up into a starry night, as she had done early this morning. Suddenly, she felt very light and was lifted from her body. She began flying around the lodge, clockwise, faster and faster, feeling as if the giant wings were her own. Then she began to feel dizzy, but she could not stop herself, as if she were propelled by some unknown source. Suddenly she was pulled back into her body by a deep "HO."

The door was opened again, and she found that she was breathing hard. Hank looked over to her and asked, "Are you okay? Is it too hot for you?"

She shook her head no, not knowing which question

to answer and not sure she could actually speak. She looked at the others to see if they were as aroused as she was and stopped when she got to Reno. He was staring at her. She thought by his look that he was aware of what she was experiencing. He nodded to her and she tried to crack a little smile as she used her towel to wipe the perspiration that was dripping from her nose and chin.

The door was closed quickly, with little time to cool down, and the heat and prayers began again. There were times when she thought she could take no more and was ready to beg Hank to let her out. Then there were times of wonderful intensity and release, strange visions, and inspiring prayers. After four rounds they finished, and Hank poured the last of the water on the rocks with a final burst of steam. They left the lodge, clockwise, into the morning light. She wrapped herself in her towel and, feeling weak and fevered, lay down on the grass in the sun, breathing deeply of the fragrant mountain air. She felt relaxed, as if she could sleep all day, and dreamily closed her eyes, glad that she had endured the entire ceremony.

A voice pulled her out of her mood, "Best be staying awake," Reno said. "You have a long day ahead of you, and we must leave soon."

She looked up and nodded, "Okay, but give me a minute." Then, remembering, she asked him, "Did you feel that bird in the lodge too? I was sure when I looked at you that you had seen the same thing."

"A bird?" Reno questioned, "you must have been feeling the eagle wing that my father was moving the air with. Things can get very confusing in the heat and darkness."

She felt as if she could trust him, so she said, "I felt a bird, and then I became the bird. I was flying around the lodge."

"Wow, that's interesting. Must have been quite a feeling. The spirits have been working on you," Reno explained. "And as for looking at you, I was just thinking how beautiful you were, sitting there all sweaty and breathing hard."

She looked up, surprised and self-conscious, and attempted to fix her tousled hair.

Reno laughed out loud, a laugh from deep within his throat, a laugh she would come to love. He gave her a wink. "Time to get dressed," he said, and walked away, towel wrapped around his waist.

Oh boy, she thought, whatever will I do? I can't have a man in my life now, there's too much else to do. But if I get well, she pondered, then maybe? No! Don't even think about it.

Rising to get dressed, she glanced over at Reno, and realized truthfully that she would have trouble resisting this one.

Chapter Fifteen

Climbing the mountain wasn't easy. She felt so weak from the sweat that she wasn't sure she could make it. And carrying Harris didn't make it any easier. Awkwardly, he sat perched on her forearm, squawking with discomfort every time she bounced around. She had borrowed Reno's jeans jacket to have something to cover her arm for Harris to stand on, and it was uncomfortably warm in the late morning sun.

Hank and Reno had joined her for the ascent, and their unwavering support was what convinced her to continue. On a normal day she would have welcomed the climb, but today the trek was torture.

Upon reaching the top, she found that the climb had been quite well worth it. What an incredibly beautiful spot! You could see for miles in all directions — white, snow-capped mountains to the west and north, plains to the east. She understood why this was the chosen place for vision quests, for as well as being visually spectacular, there was a natural wind-block in the form of a rock outcropping. It was a beautiful array of moss-covered rock with huge indentations in it, some of them big enough to be bathtubs. These depressions were filled with rainwater and Hank said a variety of birds came to bathe in them regularly.

Hank and Reno set her up on the east end of the

rocks, the highest point, so that she could see the sunrise. Hank directed her to walk around a certain area and to sit down in a spot that felt right. She eventually decided on a place that was backed by a large boulder. She liked to know what was behind her.

Hank handed her pipe to her, along with her necklace and a blanket, and unrolled the ball of pouches that they had tied yesterday. He carefully created a circle with them around her and Harris, to define the space where she was to spend the next four days. He warned her to stay inside the designated space, for this was where her protection lay. She could leave only to relieve herself. They also decided to let her keep her clothes, as the nights were getting chilly. Knowing her fragile condition, they didn't want it to be unbearable for her.

The sun was had climbed high into the sky when Hank and Reno prepared to leave. Reno watched her, sitting there on the mountain, looking so vulnerable. He went to her, offering her some valuable advice from experience.

"Think positively. Know in your heart that you can make it. When you get scared, repeat over and over some familiar name. Think of my hand holding yours. And breathe deeply. Trust. Allow yourself to cry and be healed. Our prayers are with you, your guardians are with you, the Great Spirit is with you. Remember where your strength lies."

He smiled, and then spoke quietly so only she could hear, "I love you."

She felt grateful and reassured as he spoke, yet her arms ached to reach out and hug him. But the circle was closed, so she just sat and listened, eyes shining.

Hank approached, and Reno stood up before she had a chance to say anything. Hank told her that he would be up the next morning, and both men began walking away. She attempted a smile and waved, sad to see them leave. Before the two men were out of sight, Reno turned and said, "Oh yeah, I forgot to tell you one thing. Have fun!"

She could hear both men laughing as they descended the mountain, so she yelled out, "Don't you worry, I will!"

What a couple of clowns, she thought. They never stop joking, do they? She looked questioningly at Harris and, taking a deep breath, decided to make herself comfortable. She shook out the blanket and spread it in the small space, then lay down in the sun's warmth. The sun was now high overhead, and she figured it must be well past noon.

Harris strutted around impatiently and, knowing he was hungry, she stroked him soothingly. "You are on your own for the next few days, my friend," she spoke as if he understood. "You are going to have to fix your wing and hunt if you want to eat tonight." Harris just stood there blinking, enjoying the attention and the mountain top.

She closed her tired eyes, cuddled Harris in one arm, and gave way to slumber. The past two days' events had finally caught up with her and she welcomed the chance to sleep.

▶ ◀

She awoke with a start from a dreamy, deep sleep, and was unsure of where she was. Quickly remembering, she found Harris still by her side. She sat up and realized that the sun was now in the western sky. It was almost dark, she thought with a twinge of fear. And here I am, on the most beautiful place on Earth. Alone. Well, I am not really alone. I have Harris and Harris has me, and there are trees and this great rock that I am sitting on. One can never truly be alone. The world was created full of things so that we would never get lonely. She began to talk to everything in sight, and spent most of the evening telling stories and singing familiar tunes. It made her feel at home and it took her mind off the approaching darkness. Soon she was friends with every tree and rock around her, and had a long conversation with a blue jay bathing in the rocks. She felt a kinship with all nature.

A rumble in her stomach reminded her that it was time for dinner. Not today, she patted her sunken belly. She felt uncomfortable just sitting with herself, and tried to keep her mind occupied with silly thoughts and games. Hours later, when all this had failed and she had run out of things to do, she finally sat still.

Cross-legged and upright, in the darkness of the evening, an owl by her side, she closed her eyes to meditate. Visions of past days flipped through her mind, like clippings from an old black-and-white movie. She had trouble quieting her mind, for all of her thoughts wanted her undivided attention. Pictures of Reno kept coming up. She wasn't sure what to think about him. She felt so attracted to him, his directness, his gentleness, his ability to laugh at any time, and his deep blue eyes. How in the world did a man like him ever end up with eyes like those? she wondered. She would have to ask him. She felt safe and content just thinking about him.

He's such a character, she thought. I wonder what he sees in me, a worn-out old maid. He told me he loved me, she recalled, as if she had almost forgotten, but he knows so little about me. And I just sat there and said nothing. Well, I could have said, "I love you too," but I'm not sure if I do love him. The timing was off. She felt like a schoolgirl again. Why does he always seem to be one step ahead of me?

Picturing his long black hair flying loosely in the morning breeze, she felt a desire she had ignored for years. She had purposely stayed away from all men since her fiance had died, and this new desire was summoning up feelings that had long since been buried. Deep inside she hoped to get married, but that was some day and that some day was far away. She wondered if Reno had ever been married. She hoped not. After denying her feelings for so long, it was a relief to just ponder the possibilities. She dared not hope too much, but it gave her something to dream about. And she had time on her hands.

Thoughts came and went, hunger came and stayed, and the sunset was spectacular over the ridge to her right. She shifted positions to watch the bright reds and oranges turn into blues and grays, and felt a glimmer of sadness when it was all over. There was a chill in the night air, so she cuddled up with Harris in her blanket, the pipe cradled between them.

Harris was having a hard time without any food, as he was used to eating every day since he had been with her. She had to soothe him just to keep him nearby. She was beginning to think that she shouldn't have brought him at all.

What if he wanders off while I'm asleep? she thought with a frown. Hank said there were no predators up here, but he meant predators for me — he didn't say anything about Harris. She heard the bark of a coyote down in the valley, and her fears intensified. Moving closer to Harris, she decided that she would have to stay up all night to keep an eye on him.

Then she felt a little foolish. She was basically a novice to life in the woods. Harris was born and raised out here, and here she was protecting him. It was unnatural, but she had no choice. She had made him dependent and now she would have to pay the price.

She was relieved that one day was over. Her dry, cottony mouth had made her thirst very apparent. Her stomach was rumbling and the rocky ground was hard. But she was alive. One had to look at the bright side. And no matter how committed she was to protecting Harris, drowsiness won her over and she drifted off into a deep, dreamless slumber.

Now, Harris had quite a different night. He stayed wide awake, his little owl eyes blinking at the moonless sky. With familiar sounds and scents around, he began hooting loudly. He stayed close by her side, though, aware of his limitations, and kept a nighttime vigil.

Chapter Sixteen

When we can find no distinction between dreaming and living, when our spirits fall prey to the imaginations of our minds, the black and white of reality becomes a grayish color with no real boundaries, and we find ourselves doing things we would not normally do. The vision quest ritual tends to draw us into this state of consciousness. The lack of food and water, the unfamiliar surroundings, the vulnerability, create a certain fear deep inside our core.

Now this is not an unbearable fear, it is just enough to spark the curiosity. And with the arrival of fear, irrational thinking follows, and we ponder on things that are usually forgotten. So, with this whole process, we open ourselves to instinctual behavior, yearning to find our connection with all life.

Yes, the body suffers, and withdrawals are apparent, but without having to use up precious energy by digesting food, that unused power is donated to the now absorbent spirit and mind to increase their enhancement of all they perceive. It is a process not commonly attempted, for those weak in spirit would surely suffer with no rewards, yet during healing crises, when those involved are already on the edge of life, the quest can give them the opportunity to go to the depths of their beings and discover the true cause of their diseases, directing them on paths to recovery.

The soul holds the answer to all our problems, if we would but ask the right questions and then listen carefully, for many times the answer is something we don't want to hear. Questioning is good, but listening is essential, and that is truly what a quest is: listening to the soul in total trust, alone, in peace and quiet, so that there are no distractions. Precious Mother Earth assists, nourishing us in the palm of her hand with spectacles of wonder and beauty to increase the joy that we feel at living, which urges us on to know that there is something out there, beyond, larger and more powerful than ourselves, speaking its wisdom through the trees and the sky. We agree that there must be a plan to the passage of days, and we feel part of it. Then life takes on new meaning and it seems worth fighting for.

And so, this is where we find her, stroking her little guru owl, contemplating the lack of direction in her life, fear curdled up inside, ears wide open, listening and waiting.

▶ ◀

The morning was very windy, a dry, balmy wind that blew in fast from the northwest. The sky was absent of any clouds. She figured that they had all been blown to the other side of the world. Looking up at the incredibly blue horizon, she watched as two large birds circled, and then hung in the air, motionless, on a gust. She decided they were hawks, although she really had no idea, but they were not black like crows, and she figured that eagles were too rare and would be much larger. Whatever they were, they were very graceful, dancing on the wind that she resisted and tried to escape as it blew dust into her squinting eyes.

Harris seemed to be taking it well and had sought shelter close to the big rock that she had chosen to sit by. She was relieved to find Harris there when she woke up, as she had slept heavily all night despite her long afternoon nap, not paying much attention to protecting her friend. He looked as if he were watching the birds too, and she wondered if he were wishing he could join them. She still felt apprehensive at the thought of him leaving. He had become her best friend and she enjoyed the silence of his company. He seemed to speak a language all his own, one she had begun to understand, a telepathic rapport without words. She could sense his thoughts, and know when he felt danger, when he was hungry, or when to just leave him alone. She also knew he could sense all these things in her. It was a communication that she had been unaware of at first, that had developed slowly out of need and respect for each other.

Almost three months had passed since the day they had collided, but it was a short time to become so dependent on each other. She had been learning a lot from this bird, other than the joy of friendship. He had instilled in her a very deep respect for nature. She was not absolutely sure how he had done this, she just knew that after he had arrived, she had paid more attention to small details such as the moon's phases, the direction of the wind, the placement of trees related to water, the wildflowers, the snakes. She had developed a deeper concern for everything that transpired outside her door. Even her fear of spiders had diminished, for, rather than squishing them every time she saw them, she would instead carefully watch their movements and web-spinning abilities, and admire the perfection with which they did their work. She was taught by Harris without really knowing that she was learning.

Funny, she thought, but that is why I have felt he is my teacher. He never actually teaches me anything, he just conveys his personal esteem for all of nature by being attentive, being aware of its many processes, and being in harmony with them. It is amazing how much we can learn without words.

Then, remembering a quote, she spoke out loud to Harris:

> "You don't even need to leave your room.
> Remain sitting at your table and listen.
> Don't even listen, simply wait.
> Don't even wait. Be quite still and solitary.
> The world will freely offer itself to you.
> To be unmasked it has no choice.
> It will roll in ecstasy at your feet."

"That was a little poem by Franz Kafka, but it sure says a lot," she said to the owl, "Don't you agree with me, my little feathered friend?"

She was sure Harris nodded a yes, and she laughed out loud at the serious expression on his face. "Don't owls ever laugh?" she continued, chuckling. She was startled by a voice.

"You two seem to be having fun up here. Would you like some company?" It was Reno, breathing heavily, coming over the back side of the mountain.

"Oh, hello Reno," she called, "I'm surprised to see you over there."

"Well, when you've climbed this mountain as many times as I have, it's fun to vary the route. There are so many beautiful places all around here, and the hike is a little easier on the back side, but just a bit longer," he said, catching his breath. "What a fine day. Not a cloud in the sky."

"Yes," she agreed, "the wind seems to have swept the clouds away. We had a few very strong gusts up here early this morning."

"Father and I were worried about you when the wind picked up, but we figured the rocks would protect you. Still, you are on the top of the mountain, and it can come at you from all directions. Were you cold?" Reno asked her with concern.

"Nope," she explained, "Harris kept me warm. And the wind seemed almost like an ocean breeze — rather warm and damp."

Hank was going to come up, Reno explained, but got a call from a very sick friend and needed to go doctor her, so he sent a message that he would be up tomorrow. Reno inquired as to how she was doing.

She replied, "I really don't feel very hungry right now, but my stomach was having a fit last night. It kind of comes and goes. I do feel weak and I have a small headache, but other than that I feel totally refreshed from having slept outside all night. Harris is getting quite an appetite, though, and I'm not sure if he can make it for three more days without food. He doesn't really understand the cosmic possibilities of fasting," she explained with a smile. "I keep getting the feeling that he will wander off at night looking for something to eat."

"I'm sure Harris is having a hard time," Reno agreed, "but I doubt he will leave you unless he can fly. He is aware of his vulnerability." Reno reached his hand out to the bird. "He really is a beautiful creature. It's not often that one gets to see an owl this close up."

They sat in the windy morning sun together, talking of owls and nature and friends. She learned much about Reno. His mother had died when he was five years old — she had been part Spanish and part German, with beautiful bronze skin and vivid blue eyes. He couldn't remember much about her — just the stories his father had told him. He also had a couple of treasured photos. So that was where his peculiar eyes came from. His father had remarried soon afterwards to Sheila, and then his brother Steve was born. There were only two children. He had been able to get a scholarship and go to college to study art, and made a living primarily from his carvings and artwork.

She shared a little of her childhood, and they found that they had come from completely different worlds. They found that they each envied the things which the other one disliked. They were a peculiar combination, but they somehow balanced each other. Reno had been married years ago, but had divorced after three years, and hadn't had the courage to attempt it again. That was, until he had met her. He didn't verbally display his ambitions, but it was evident in his gaze and his actions.

Sensing his attraction, she warned him, "I don't know why you love me, Reno. I'm a jinx. You better keep your distance from me. My bad luck may be contagious." She bit her lower lip nervously.

"Well, I usually have good luck, so maybe we'll be good for each other," Reno said optimistically with a smile.

"I really feel close to you Reno, but I'm afraid. I'm not sure I can let myself fall in love with you — or anyone for that matter. I don't want to get involved and then die. It wouldn't be fair to either of us," she explained sadly.

Reno understood her dilemma, but tried to be positive, "I'm willing to take my chances. It's been so long since I've cared for a woman and there is something about you that intrigues me. I'm not sure what it is, but, umm," he stuttered, unsure, then spit out, "I would like to help you get well."

"Oh Reno, I want to get well," she said enthusiastically. "I can't really believe this is happening. I certainly don't feel intriguing, but I am drawn to you as well. It may just take some time for me to get used to the idea of being close to another person again."

"You have the rest of your life," he responded happily, and placing his hand on his heart he recited dramatically, "It's better to have loved and died, than not to have loved at all."

She laughed calmly, then rolled her eyes to the sky and replied jokingly, "And you my friend, are a little bit crazy."

The sun was high in the sky when Reno stood up and stretched his arms to the sky, informing her and Harris that he had to be on his way. "I'd love to sit up here all day, but I do have work to do. Not all of us have it this easy," he said teasingly, breaking the romantic mood. "Are you sure you'll be okay? I'd hate to have anything happen to you." He smiled at her brightly, "You really look like you belong up here — another beautiful piece of Mother Nature's work." He stood back to examine her, and she blushed under his gaze.

"I am very happy you came to visit us. We enjoyed your company," she spoke honestly. Standing up in her circle, she parted the string of pouches and walked out to watch him leave. Her legs wobbled from stiffness and she reached to the closest rock for support.

He approached her quickly, asking, "Are you sure you'll be all right?"

She nodded, a half smile on her face, and their eyes locked in a silent gaze. "You have a Mona Lisa smile," he spoke to her, "that I can't resist." He took her face in his hands, cupped her chin, and gave her a long and gentle kiss.

"Please be careful," was all he said as he turned slowly and walked down the mountain, leaving an empty space on the rocks.

She was quivering, excited. Her arms hung limply at her sides while she licked the fresh moistness from her parched lips and stood lingering in the magnificence of true love's first kiss. Her life had now taken on new meaning. She was surprised that she could feel so much love.

Both she and the man spent much of the day thinking about each other, their hearts locked in anticipation, wondering what was to become of their attraction and desire.

► ◄

The afternoon passed quickly, and at sunset she held her pipe up to the heavens and prayed, "O Great Spirit, thank you for bringing me here. Please guide me to my vision, so that I may become well in my body and in my heart. My desire to live is now stronger than ever before. My heart is open and I offer myself to you for direction. Please show me the way. Where is my home? There must be someplace I belong, someplace where I can fit in and help others. I yearn to have purpose to my days. I have wasted so many years already. Cleanse me of the past so that I may be free to enjoy the future. Heal my wounds. Thank you, Mother Earth, for your protection. You are a kind and gentle mother, always giving. Teach me to be as loving and compassionate as you are."

She lay down next to Harris, and placed her head on the warm ground. She wept, slowly at first, then breaking into deep sobs of release. Her tears of pain trickled out onto the Earth, and were absorbed as nourishment. It was there that she fell asleep, distraught but secure, gently cradled in her mother's breast.

Chapter Seventeen

She had a dream that shook her to the core. It was so real that she had a difficult time convincing herself that it was only in her mind. She was never sure where to draw the imaginary line with dreams, and when to accept them as reality, as viable experience. This dream stepped over the usual boundaries. It dissolved the line between imaginary and absolute. Both qualities seemed to join together into a category all its own, defining new possibilities. She was excited at the prospect.

▶ ◀

She was flying, flying with ease in a world that she had never remembered being so beautiful. The colors were absolutely brilliant and intense, and everything vibrated with a radiant life source. Over hills and valleys she flew, following a winding dirt path below her.

She seemed to fly with incredible speed, flashing by but totally aware of every rock and flower. She was astonished but relaxed, and continued with great confidence, as if she knew exactly where she was going.

Off to her left was a giant boulder, and as she approached it, it changed its form into the face of an old bearded man. It was a large head, emerging fully with a smile as old as life itself. At first surprised and fearful of this giant being, she then looked into his eyes and sensed an abundance of peace and wisdom. An arm now appeared out of the rock and pointed down the path, giving her direction.

She slowed and thanked him with a wordless nod of her head, and he smiled so radiantly that it overwhelmed her with love. She considered staying, only for a moment, but knew that she had to move on in the direction he had pointed.

Flying speedily, she soon approached an immense building. It was a gigantic sort of castle, shimmering brightly in a valley to her right. She landed by the entryway, and two enormous, stately, golden doors opened silently by themselves. Admitting herself to this massive palace, eyes trying to absorb the magnificence around her, she felt as small and as insignificant as a mouse. She explored considerately, stepping lightly, then stopped suddenly in the center of the room.

Directly in front of her appeared a circular staircase — brilliant, glistening — spiraling up into a blue mist. It beckoned her with its glory and she began ascending the steps, slowly and with purpose, curious as to what lay above. When she reached the landing, she found herself in a small room with a glass-domed roof. In the center of the room, three women sat quietly around a small, round table. The moon shone in clearly through the dome, dispelling the mist, and bathing their bodies in a beautiful, golden glow. The women offered her a place to sit and, facing north, she joined the group, gracefully descending onto a low wooden bench. She had never remembered meeting any of the women previously, yet sensed a familiarity in their eyes and felt that she completed the circle. No one spoke. All eyes were focused on the bright lights that were embedded in the table. Following suit, she explored the illuminated objects to try to understand the significance they held. Three miniature stars formed a distinct triangle in the middle of the table, and each star had a name written by it: Altair, Deneb, Vega. The moon seemed to be the source that illuminated the stars, although she could not be absolutely sure. The moment lingered, somehow timeless.

The women then placed their hands palms up on the table in the middle of the triangle. She did the same. One woman, with silver hair and eyes of fire, spoke like water would speak, flowing and irresistible, a sentence of words that was so foreign to her that she knew she could never remember them. After the woman repeated it four times, the dome lit up and a dazzling white light flashed through the room, blinding them all. When she was finally able to see, she looked at the triangle of hands and each pair was holding a ball of light, a glorious, glowing globe, whose edges could not be defined. She accepted hers with reverence, and carefully cradled it in her hands. She searched the ball for details and found that it radiated far beyond its edges. It had no weight, yet it had form and density. Its brilliance hypnotized her and she felt charged by the dazzling light.

▶ ◀

That was all she remembered as she woke up to find her hands illuminated, her palms glowing like the sphere that had now disappeared. She felt no heat in her hands;

they just seemed to be charged and vibrating slightly. She observed them with excitement, glad that her dream had crossed over into her waking state. She continued to stare at her hands for an hour, until the brilliance diminished and all she could feel was the tingling left behind.

What an incredible dream, she thought, as she tried to remember every detail so that it would be permanently etched in her mind. There was more significance to this dream than she thought she could absorb in one sitting and she wanted to retain it for another time.

It was barely morning as she sat on the rock, palms glowing, eyes dancing with the first twinkling of the dawn. She pulled her blanket closer, covering her shoulders and trying to ward off the chill, as she felt a surge of real joy. She felt truly happy inside, undeniably excited about the future, as if her prayers had been answered. Was it the dream, or being on the mountain top at sunrise, or just the pure passion of life? She hadn't felt this way since childhood. Not that her childhood had been all that incredible. It was just that she was starting to re-embody the wonderful lightness and playfulness that she had as a child.

Feeling ecstatic, she stood up, stretched her stiff limbs, and began to dance. It was a slow, gentle movement that she had learned from the women at the moon lodge. Breathing rhythmically, she crouched, then gradually rose and drew the Earth's energy upward with her hands towards the sky. Then, drawing the ball of energy downward, she pulled it into her belly, inhaling, and with a swift kick she shoved it out towards the east. She performed this motion towards each of the four directions, feeling empowered and in her center.

She sensed a wholeness within her, as if all her functions were synchronized, performing together in unison, a concerted effort. She felt as if the cancer would melt away under the gleaming splendor of her heart. She knew that if she could keep up this positiveness, this aura of light that she had achieved, anything would be possible.

She also knew that becoming whole was a long process. That wholeness was developed through balancing the mind, emotions, body, and spirit. They each have a direct effect on the other. If the scale is tipped to one side, if one element is undernourished, the imbalance compensates by forcing a condition that demands attention. In her case it was cancer. Emotionally cut off, spiritually depressed, and mentally overworked, her body had simply revolted. As a human cell is a whole structure, it requires whole foods to rebuild itself. If food has been processed, and consists of only part of its original form, it can only reconstruct a portion of the cell. The world was created with wisdom and people must act with it. Whole foods were created for a reason: to be eaten as they were conceived. Convenience has destroyed our sensibilities, and thus our health.

She understood it to be the same case with emotions. In order to function sanely, we must, as children, observe and experience a healthy emotional parent or guardian. If we have been neglected emotionally, or denied a chance to act with honesty, the delicate growth of our image is severely stunted. The sensitive wholeness is then damaged. This process is the same with our spirits and our minds. Ignoring any one aspect of our beings results in chaos.

But she knew she could not allow her losses as a young

child, or even as an adult, to ruin her entire life. The desire to change was inevitable and it was actually her saving grace, demanding that she rearrange her habits and actions towards a more balanced interaction with her everyday affairs. All people have the ability to change. Working towards wholeness in each faction of our beings, and then merging them into a healthy whole, serves to enhance our relationships and to cure our dis-eases. It allows us to live with real joy.

She had reached these crossroads on her journey, as each of her four essences was striving to put the pieces of her puzzle back together in a harmonious setting. Consequently, she had become a child once again. She had to return to the beginning, where the pain had originated. The freshness of her consciousness wanted to erase the painful memories, to start with a clean slate, but they were a constitutional part of her essence and she could no more leave them behind than she could her merry blue eyes. It was necessary to use her misfortunes as stepping stones towards wholeness. Revealed, and hence no longer feared, they now gave her character substance rather than suffering.

She laughed out loud and finished her graceful dance on the top of the world, pleased that she had figured out what her life was all about, at least for this moment in time. Her theories might change, like the shifting of the winds, but the relief and joy she felt in her heart would remain forever. We must each, sometime during life, decide to live for our own reasons. She was doing it for the pure thrill of it all.

Chapter Eighteen

 Her stomach clenched into a knot as the warming rays of the morning sun enveloped her tiny world. Harris was gone! She stood up and gazed in every direction, hopeful eyes attempting to get a sighting of the owl. But he was nowhere to be seen, and she knew it was against the rules to leave the mountain top.

Flopping to the ground in desperation, she clutched the necklace that Reno had given her, and sighed. She had known that Harris would leave sooner or later, and they had been there two nights already; how could she have expected him to resist the night world of the forest? It was his home. She just hoped and prayed that he was okay.

Thinking back to her dreams and thoughts, she felt as if she had received some sort of mysterious healing. A true change had taken place during the night. She wondered if Harris had experienced a similar healing, and was now able to fly. How wonderful it would be if that were true! It was as if they had both been given wings, and had been set free from self-imposed cages. It was almost more than she could hope for. A poem formed in her mind and she spoke it out loud:

> I dreamed we were flying
> in the light of the moon

> You were the pilot
> and I was the wings
> An oasis of clouds
> adrift in the light
> We sailed on as one
> hearts merged in delight
> I awoke in the knowing
> that dreams are not real
> But the song that we carry
> is the melody that I feel

"Oh Harris, where are you?" she called to an empty sky. She knew she had to let go, to allow him the same freedom that she strived for, but her heart ached and she was lonely. She opened the circle, and stepped out to walk around and stretch her legs. Maybe he was wandering around on the rocks?

She explored close by, not wanting to stray too far from her chosen spot. She searched for owl feathers to see if, perchance, there had been any sort of struggle. To her relief and to her dismay, she saw nothing.

Feeling weak and nauseous, she returned to the circle to sit. Even though it felt good to move around, she was going on her third day with no food and it was taking its toll. Her head ached sharply over her eyes, her neck was suddenly stiff, and the movement had made her very light-headed. It certainly affected her much differently than the dancing had.

She closed her eyes and sat up straight, trying to breathe

deeply and relax. She tried to tell herself that she shouldn't be so upset. She wanted to feel good again, happy and playful, but she had opened the door to her heart and Harris' departure had triggered the release of past memories of her fiance's death, a memory she had stuffed deep inside. She couldn't quite understand the process behind what was happening, and how the two were related.

She felt very disoriented and suddenly confused, as if the past few days had melted into each other. She could sense no distinction between then and now. She tried to shake the feeling, as she felt she was losing touch with reality. And she was.

She drifted helplessly, without control, her mind aimlessly wandering through memories of the past and present: her childhood, her Grandfather, her parents, Harris, Reno, her fiance, her job; they all swirled and mingled into one emotional stew pot. It was both enjoyable and distressing. A melancholy mood settled on her as she attempted to put it all in order.

She was not sure how long this feeling pervaded her psyche, but she was revived by a gentle voice calling her name. She struggled to respond, pulling herself out of the somber state, and cracked her eyelids to find Hank staring at her, a concerned expression on his wrinkled, leathery face. Feeling as if she had been caught unguarded, she shook her hair back, flustered, and forced a smile. An unpleasant quivering remained in her belly.

"Are you okay?" Hank asked anxiously, as he opened the circle and touched her hand.

"Yes, I think so. I just, well, I kind of lost touch there for a minute. But, I think I'm fine now."

Hank searched her eyes to discover the truth, but found that they were blank. She herself was not even sure what had transpired. Hank glanced around suddenly, asking, "Where's Harris?" Then, realizing what was going on, he said, "Did he fly off last night?"

She shook her head up and down silently as the thought filled her eyes with tears. Then, brushing them off with a shake of her head, she replied, "I'm not sure what happened to him. I woke up this morning and he was gone. I've looked all around the mountain top and can find no sign of him. I feel so guilty for not taking better care of him. If he's dead it's my fault. What can I do? I feel so helpless."

Hank sat down next to her and began to speak, with a stern look on his face. "Life and death in nature is very different from what we believe it to be. All living things have their time in life. They do not desire, as we do, to live a very long time, advancing into old age with all the miracles of modern medicine to keep us alive. They would have worn out their welcome. In the wild, only the strong survive.

"They are content to live and have offspring and die. Life is simple. Of course they fight for life if they need to. Each living thing has the desire to continue living, but there is a difference. The death of one animal becomes the continuation of life for another. They are supported on a delicate balance and no one is more important than the next.

"Humans destroy this balance. How many animals are killed when the rain forests are destroyed? How many turkeys die every Thanksgiving just so that we can enjoy a feast? How many insects are smashed on the hood of your car every time you drive to town? Thousands are killed every day and no one mourns for them; it is useless to cry over one single owl. If you truly care, you must mourn for each and every one.

"And, for all we know, Harris may be alive, flying free and cured, and we should be rejoicing."

She listened to him carefully and with respect, and then replied, "I understand what you are saying, but I don't know every animal and bird. I had the rare opportunity to get close to a beautiful creature and he was my responsibility. I've nursed him along for so long, and he, in turn, has been my teacher. Now that he's gone, well, I feel at a loss. I'm having trouble controlling my emotions. I feel somehow, uh, well, desperate. My heart aches."

She burst out crying with a scream that she could no longer hold back. The sobbing racked her body and she felt very confused. A myriad of emotions were wrestling to become the most important: fear, anger, self-pity, perplexity; they each strived for recognition.

"And you know, Hank, this morning I awoke from an incredible dream. It left me feeling so happy, so amazingly light. I really thought I had been healed. But now, the pain is overwhelming again. It's as if I am at the mercy of these invisible feelings. They seem to overpower me, and I hate it!" she exclaimed, sulking and sniffling.

Hank put his arm around her to ease the suffering. She laid her head weakly in his lap while he stroked her hair and comforted her as if she were his own daughter. He began to chant an old Indian song, slowly and deeply. The rhythm caressed her, and it lulled her mind towards peace.

Hank spoke to her, forcefully, "There is much pain and

resentment that is surfacing from deep within you. Layers of grief have built up on your soul, and you must peel them off slowly, so that the pain is not unbearable. Each cleansing will allow you to feel more alive, freer than you ever imagined. Soon, the grief will have dissipated and your heart will be lighter. Your whole being will rejoice. The process is long but worthwhile, so please endure, my daughter, and soon all will be clear. The more you know the more you will realize.

"Death will sit before you for many more years, unguarded, inevitable, while your healing takes place. But death is not something to fear either. You must look beyond it, to the other side of life, the side that accepts us all.

"There is a part of you that keeps your heart beating, that takes you dreaming, that connects you with all other life. It is called spirit, the essence of your being. Your spirit never dies. When you lose your body, the clothing of the spirit, you are free to fly, to explore realms more beautiful than anything you have seen here on Earth. And you will not be alone — your relatives will be there to meet you, the angels will guide you, and you will wonder why you were ever scared of dying.

"The Great Spirit is merciful and seeks only to raise you up, gently. The world above is as this world below, and you will find it very familiar and enjoyable.

"So, really, you have nothing to fear except your fear itself. Whether your body lives or dies, your essence will live on. Overcome your resistance to something that you have no power over and you will be at ease, and a lot happier as well."

Hank smiled widely as she sat up, rubbing her eyes and brushing her hair out of her face. "Thank you Hank, I feel much better now. What you have said makes a lot of sense. It reminds me of my dream last night. The place that I traveled to was very vibrant and beautiful, just as you have described." She gave Hank a brief description of the dream, the room, the globe of light, and the triangle of stars.

Hank considered her words and then pointed to the sky, saying, "There is a triangle of stars called the 'summer triangle', and it consists of the three stars you mentioned. Look to the heavens tonight, directly in the center of the sky, and you will view the lights. These certain stars are only visible here during the summer. The spirits have given you a waking dream. This is a good sign. You hold the light of the future in the palms of your hands. Use it wisely."

"Oh, I will try, Hank. I'm not sure I deserve this, but I'll do my best. Can you forgive me for getting so carried away?" she asked softly.

Hank replied, "Oh, please don't apologize to me. You have done nothing wrong. The truth is sometimes the hardest thing to find. Most of us are so confused, so fearful of death, that we choose not to explore it. It is too painful, so it remains veiled in mystery. In my culture, death is talked of more openly, so we are free of its mystery, and we have a great respect for it. The transition is easier. We still mourn of course, but not for the dead; we mourn for ourselves as we are the ones who are left behind.

"Now, young one, I must be going. Make peace with yourself and your Creator, and have faith that you are walking the right path. And remember, life is for enjoying! Don't take it all so seriously!"

Hank burst out laughing, stood up, and patted her on the head. "We will talk more about all this later. See you tommorrow," Hank said, waving as he climbed over the rocks and down the mountain, leaving her in the element she desired most: solitude.

She sat exhausted, as still as one of the mountain-top rocks. Her mind was full of ideas. What can life be like when I die? she thought carefully. Is it even life at all? Can life up there really be a mirror of this existence? Is it even up there at all? she wondered as she gazed towards the sky. Is the spirit world beautiful, as Hank said it was? Can it be like my dream? Was I in the heavens last night?

She had heard so many different ideas. Every religion seemed to have its own theory: heaven and hell, reincarnation, judgment day; why couldn't they all agree? And now there was Hank's concept, a sane and logical explanation. Somehow she felt comfortable with it. She mulled over the information in her mind and hoped Hank's belief was the truth. But how was one ever to know for sure until they had died?

Considering the power of a thought, she wondered if what we believe is actually what happens to us. If we believe that we have sinned and will be put in hell, will we be? If we believe that the Creator is fair and forgiving and that we can make up for our mistakes and be blessed for it on the other side, will we be? This thought opened up a whole new avenue of her imagination.

If we are what we eat, then are we what we think we are? Is death what we decide it will be? Do we each experience the reality of our own minds? Or, is there some overseeing intelligence that has its own set of laws that blows every theory that the human race has ever conceived of?

There must be a set of universal laws that governs all, she decided, just as gravity affects all, and it is our lives' work to determine what these laws are and to become in harmony with them. This makes perfect sense. That must be why nature and animals are able to react so appropriately — because they are in harmony with those laws. Why then are humans not endowed with this same gracious gift?

Her mind swirled with the formation of the ideas presented to her. Each thought seemed to conflict with the next and she wondered if she would have to die to find the truth. That might be it, she thought. That would give some purpose to death, some renewing factor that would make the passage to another plane worthwhile. Well, at least I have something to look forward to, she chuckled silently, remembering Hank's plea for less seriousness.

Death seemed more of a friend, now that it had offered something to her. She resolved that she would not concern herself with death anymore, as it held many questions that she could not answer, but that she would focus on living, healthfully and consciously, and helping those around her to enjoy life. She wanted the rest of her life to be valuable and worthwhile. She pondered on what her newly chosen profession could be, and said a small prayer for guidance.

A world of opportunities seemed to sit before her in display, all offering their own rewards. She had recovered from the pain once again. Another layer was gone. This was all very exciting, and life was truly amazing, but her weakened and hungry body moaned for rest, so she closed her sleepy eyes and drifted like an autumn leaf through the delightful world of anticipation.

Finally, she had enough faith to realize that her destiny would present itself to her when the time was right. She wondered if it would have anything to do with those golden, healing globes. It really didn't matter. She was one of those persons who always had everything she needed, even when she didn't realize it.

Chapter Nineteen

The third day of her quest passed slowly, to her delight, as her thoughts meandered patiently like a warm summer's creek through the muck and mud of the world's offerings. It was not a struggle, it just took a while for her to understand things. For the truth of existence to make its debut, it had to rearrange and upset most prior accepted theories that had made their homes in her absorbent mind. It had previously been difficult to let go of settled impressions, but now they gently made way for the new.

She awoke from her nap, content and rested. She stood up yawning and stretched, feeling good in her body. Wanting to take advantage of these pleasant sensations, she sat down to meditate.

With no food to digest in her belly, her energy was freed for the mental process and this allowed her to move easily into a meditative state. She sat perfectly still for hours, and once, thinking she was a statue, a robin landed on her shoulder. A calm and positive transition took place, and fluidity replaced rigidity. The past four months in the mountains had been amazing. So much had happened in such a short period of time. It was as if she had been ripened for some purpose. But she was just one sickly mortal. What difference could she make? She supposed that time would tell.

Now, she knew that her new-found flexibility would allow healing to take place. It had taken many years for the disease to develop, so it would take time for the disease to reverse itself. The process was not close to being finished, as for her it had been a lifetime occupation, but the first change was the hardest and she could finally partake of life's precious gifts without remorse in her heart. There was one thing that made all the difference in the world; she would no longer spend her time resisting death; now she would wade in the luxury of life. Soon she would be doing the backstroke. Death was there; it would always be there — a black raven perched low and defiant — but it no longer filled her with fear. Ah, but life, it was a high-flying eagle, soaring instinctively and nobly; difficult to embrace fully with its impulsive heights, but oh so desired, and liberal with its rewards.

The sun was low in the sky, but still very hot, when she finally opened her meditative eyes to find beads of perspiration on her upper lip. She didn't want to sweat; it wasted her precious moisture. She stood up to leave the circle and find a place to relieve herself, surprised that she even had to after three dry days. She had surely begun to appreciate water at this point.

Her meditation had left her mind wide open. Walking around, she began to feel slightly dizzy, but intensely clear. She looked at the skyline and noticed that the trees seemed to glow. They were outlined by a white light, and sparks appeared to be flying in all directions, originating in the thin air surrounding her — a subdued fireworks show.

It was magical. It reminded her of her dream, the

grass, the snake, and the rock giving her messages she had not then fully comprehended. Now they hit home.

"Bend with us; do not resist," the grass had spoken. It must have been trying to tell me not to resist death, to flow with the energy of the moment, she decided.

"Feel our Earth Mother beneath your belly," the serpent had shared. It was trying to explain how the Earth absorbs pain.

"All things you need are within," the rock had said, telling me that I needn't search for answers beyond my own heart.

Did I make up this dream? she asked herself. Did my spirit create these ideas? I must have, she decided. Then I probably already knew all these things. How strange, she considered. It has taken me so long to realize what I've known inside all along. These ideas have subconsciously affected my thoughts and my actions, bringing my visions into a conscious reality. My journey did go within; I have Mother Earth beneath me; I am not resisting; I have let go. How did I know that I needed these elements to heal myself?

But what was the last message? The owl had not spoken. It had been Harris. He has taught me so much without ever speaking one word, she revealed. Oh, how I miss my feathered friend, she spoke to her heart.

Then suddenly, to the south, she saw a bird hovering, its large wings hanging on the stillness of the sky. She felt as if she were in her dream once more. But this time the bird descended of its own power, swooping slowly and coming to a landing in front of her.

It was Harris! He was alive! She thought her heart would burst. Crouching down, she held out her open hand

and he pecked at it gently, looking up into her teary eyes. This woman had healed him. He would never forget her. He would be her source of instinctual power, her flying guardian. But now he must say goodbye.

She wiped the wetness from her eyes with the back of her hand so that she could clearly see this magnificent creature one last time. The owl seemed to stand much taller now that he was free and unhindered by his injury. His beak moved up and down nervously, his clawed feet shuffling like a child anxious to move. He spoke through his eyes, wide now from the unfamiliarity of the bright sun, conveying words in a form that she could never write down. He was expressing the closest thing she knew to be love, yet she was only beginning to comprehend its power. The intensity startled her. Shuddering, she would forever recall this moment as ecstatic, and never again doubt the healing power of love.

She reached out and stroked his fully healed wing, basking in the sublime joy of true friendship. She knew he had come back to say goodbye, to show her that her efforts had been worthwhile, and that all healing is possible.

He hooted once, loud and deep. Then the familiarity in his eyes faded into a savage gaze, and she instantly knew that he was no longer hers. The wild flame of nature's blazing desire had once again filled his heart and called him back. Just as it should be.

Their time together was finished, the purpose fulfilled, and he spread his giant wings and gracefully lifted himself towards the horizon, towards his home.

So long, my friend, she waved, happy that he was free at last. His freedom filled her with contentment, and she smiled, a salty tear stinging her dry, chapped lips.

► ◄

Dusk set in slowly, with an impressive array of colors — brilliant hues that tinted her reflective eyes. It was a warm evening, which pleased her, without a breeze in the air, and she looked forward to a good night's sleep. She had never been so alone, but somehow so safe and secure in the world. Here on the mountain there were no doors to lock, nothing to keep out. She no longer even needed to hide herself. Her heart had bloomed into a new spring flower, displayed for all the world to see.

She was open now and a deep honesty graced her mind. She began to think about Reno. He was like a pillar of strength and she knew she could always lean on him. And she loved him. She could finally admit that she loved him — unconditionally. She knew that they had been brought together for some purpose and that they would never be separate in spirit. She was not concerned with the future of their relationship. Of course she had her desires and knew that their bodies would mingle lusciously. She could smell the smoke of their passion. But that was only part of it. The exhilaration she felt at simply knowing that the man existed was enough to carry her forward. She would be grateful for whatever form their love took.

Words of a newly sculpted poem escaped from her lips

without much thought. It came from the heart. She named it "Simply Love":

> Simply gazing
> Into the deep blue void of your eyes
> Allows my soul to rest.
>
> Actively listening
> To the husky melody of your words
> Overcomes my fear.
>
> Gently holding
> The firm posture of your substance
> Stills my wanderings.
>
> Wildly laughing
> At the freedom you act upon
> Releases my heart.
>
> I cannot ask for more.

Now, she thought, I am truly home. I am at home in my heart. I accept myself for who I am. I have bared my soul before all these creatures and trees and they have accepted me also, returning only solitude and peace. What a gift.

She arose and went to the closest tree and hugged it hard and tight, tears trickling from her eyes to the green-gray mossy rock below. She felt so much gratitude to the Earth for accepting and dissolving her pain that she bent down and kissed the rocks, whispering, "My true mother, I love you."

Then she stood up straight and tall, and raised her arms towards the tranquil sky, embracing the air and clouds. She spoke, "Father, so expansive, I love you!"

She twirled in a circle, arms flapping like a bird, laughter in her eyes. She gave a mighty howl, like a wolf on a full moon's night, and released her appreciation to the creatures of the forest. "This is the heart of the world," she told them, "the compassionate heart of splendor, and it is my home!"

▶ ◀

Days later, as she lay in bed, a pencil clutched in one hand, and a wildflower behind her ear, her mind sifted through her four-day journey. The fourth day on the mountain had been the best. Confident and radiant, she had spent the day focusing on what to do with her life. The impact of this was now very clear. She had achieved more than she had ever hoped for: free from the shackles of self persecution, fully alive and spiritually potent, she embraced life as never before. The time to share her realizations and her experiences had come about.

She decided to write it all down. She had a talent for poetry, or so she'd been told, and she knew that it was a direct path to another's heart. She wanted to make shock waves, to collide with the world's collective mind. She wanted to make a difference.

It was dusk as she began to write down her delicate words. High above, the clouds began to speak, the thunder beings were doing a dance, and the rain trickled gently to the Earth as her sympathetic tale trickled down her fingers onto the paper. As lightning lit up the sky, it revealed an owl circling the house, rain dripping from its ample wings. She gazed up, feeling his presence, and smiled. Their story was one that needed to be told. And so it began: "A crackling fire, a booming drumbeat, the rattle of a bean-filled gourd..."

Starting Your Own Moon Lodge

The Moon Lodge ceremony, or Lodge of the Sisters as I prefer to call it, is a traditional ceremony based on an American Indian ritual. The ceremony that the members of our lodge have designed is not at all like the traditional ceremony of old, but is a revised edition that we have incorporated into our lifestyles to suit the needs of the participants. It is revitalizing and spiritually charging. It is wonderful to see growing numbers of women beginning to utilize the beauty and power that this ritual provides, its resurgence awakening a deep need within women to share with, and heal the Earth, their mother. It is by no means a denial of our male partners; rather it is an empowering experience allowing women's hearts to join, and thus add more to their families and society. Taken as growth and an increased ability to harmonize with their surroundings, many women are finding support in the Lodge of the Sisters. Following is a suggested method for starting your own Moon Lodge:

▶*Organize a small core group of dedicated women.* This group of women should be able to make it to most ceremonies. There seems to be more resonance, and more gets done, when many of the same women participate. This group can create the basic rituals and design the ceremony, and then other women who want to join, or just participate once or twice, can merge into the designated plans. Each women should share in some phase of the ceremony. It has also been our experience that no one person should be in charge. Decisions are best made democratically.

▶*Build a lodge.* This is probably the most time-consuming part, but it can also be the most fun. If one member has a large piece of land and is willing to share it, it is nice to have a lodge that is somewhat secluded. If not, I'm sure any backyard or large space will do. We have also done the ceremony in different women's living rooms, especially in winter, which is fine, just not as exciting or inspiring as doing it outside.

With the help of the men folk, our group built a six-sided, interlocked log structure, approximately ten to twelve feet in diameter and four to five feet high. The side to the east was left open for an entrance. A cone-shaped roof was put on top and shingled, with an opening in the center for the smoke to escape. It resembled a yurt. We then talked with a local adobe maker. He suggested a mixture of clay, sand, and lime that was proper for our bioregion to fill in the cracks between the interior logs to block out all light. We bought the clay from a local excavator (cheap — five dollars per truckload, and one truckload was plenty), the sand we dug up at a nearby pond, and the lime was purchased at the local hardware store in a 50-pound bag. We mixed it all in an old wheelbarrow to the proper specifications of two parts clay to one part sand to one part lime. Depending on the altitude and humidity of your area and the permanence of your structure, your mixture could be different. The adobe maker suggested using concrete in the mixture for a long-lasting base, but we opted not to because of its harsh qualities. We also learned that you must pack the adobe firmly between the logs. It is best to do this on a warm, sunny day with no possibility of frost in the following week, because the change in temperature would crack the hardening adobe. We placed blankets over the entrance to block the light, so we could see if we had any cracks left that needed to be patched with the wet mixture. Since the lodge was not large enough to stand up in, we crawled around to work. What joy it was to be on the damp ground and have my hands covered with mud! The earthy smell and warm sun shining is a memory not soon to be forgotten. We then flattened the area inside the lodge and dug a firepit in the center, about one foot deep and two feet in diameter.

Rocks placed on the bottom of the pit help to keep the fire going, to hold onto the heat on chilly nights, and to burn the herbs on. Our lodge has held up for over two years now and the adobe has only slightly cracked, but it has not fallen off. Good luck! Don't be afraid to be creative and ask for advice.

▶ *Develop a ceremony.* First, be clear about your objectives. Why are you gathering and what do you want to accomplish? Second, it is a good idea to create your activities around the spiritual beliefs of your group. Our ceremony was developed using many Native American chants and rituals, although we did not limit ourselves to these. We chose to base our activities on the four elements: air, fire, water, and earth. We wanted to incorporate each of these into our ceremonies. It gave us something tangible to work with. Sitting on the earth and burning herbs fulfilled our requirement for the earth element. For water, we always shared some water or a simple herbal tea that we had blessed. For fire, we prepared a small teepee of sticks and paper before we entered the lodge and lit it later in the ceremony, using it to smoke the herbs and to stay warm. For air, one woman led an exercise for deep breathing and centering that was performed before we lit the fire, so we would not inhale the smoke.

We also used a prayer stone, a palm-sized rock that was special to someone. Since the stone seemed to gather energy and power, we used the same one each time. We passed it in a clockwise direction, and each woman holding it offered her prayer, until the rock had completed one cycle around the lodge. It would then continue its revolutions until everyone had prayed. This ceremony took on the symbolism of the moon's cycles, changing and revolving around the lodge as the moon does around the Earth.

A variety of different instruments were used in the lodge to add rhythm to the chants as well as complexity and beautiful sounds. Drums, rattles, gourds, flutes, tambourines, or just plain clapping helped musically and invited everyone to participate. It is a good idea to be organized before entering the lodge so that the ceremony flows smoothly. Discuss the progression of activities; for example, who will be responsible for an opening prayer, a closing prayer, the herbs, a breathing exercise, a dance, a chant, the water, etc. Using these guidelines, we never seemed to have any difficulty coming up with new ideas, and the ceremonies were never the same.

▶*Focus each ceremony on a certain theme.* We found that

it was very powerful and fulfilling if all members of our group had the same intention in mind while we were praying. You may find this to be true as well. For example, the subject of one lodge might be world peace, the next might be an individual who is sick or dying. If a mother is pregnant and near birthing, she could be the focus of prayers for a healthy and easy birth experience. Use herbs and chants that are appropriate for your particular theme, so that everyone's focus will be united. The theme of one of our lodges was supporting each other in major life changes, since everyone seemed to be going through a lot of phases, and it was helpful to be putting positive energy into those changes. The options are limitless. We found it amazing that all of us would be going through similar stuff at the same time. Let it flow and have fun!

▶*Buy or make a moon chart.* It is important to know when the moon is new or full, so that you will know the proper day to have the ceremony. We chose the new moon day because it signified to us the potential for new beginnings, and we all agreed it was a powerful time. It helps us to stay in harmony with these cycles. Use your own experience and inspiration to determine which phase you will celebrate. Equinoxes, solstices, and eclipses were also special times for us and we have gotten together for them as often as possible. You can make your own moon chart from information found on calendars or astronomical charts. Or, you may purchase a Moon Calendar by Kim Long that is precise and well laid-out from S&S Optika, 5172 S. Broadway, Englewood, CO 80110. Either way, the closer your ceremony comes to the exact time of the astronomical occurrence the better, although we usually planned our ceremonies at sunset, as this was logistically easier for moms and working women.

▶*Suggested herbs.* We used dried herbs, placing them on the fire or on hot rocks to release their aromatic qualities. Fresh herbs are fine as well. A different woman was designated to bring the herbs to each lodge, using ones that seemed to best fit the theme. The herbs were passed to each woman and burned throughout the ritual. We tried to have fresh sage on the floor of the lodge each time — for seating comfort and aroma — as it is an abundant local herb in summer and autumn. Use whatever your region produces that is fresh, soft, and smells sweet. Research some medicinal herb books for appropriate suggestions. Here is a partial list of some herbs we have used and their properties:

Barberry or Bayberry — for universal love
Basil — brings fertility
Cedar — for purification of environment
Chamomile — for peace and relaxation
Horsemint (Wild Oregano) — rub on body for purification
Lavender — for birthing energy
Myrrh — for purification through crying
Pine Sap — for centering and stress reduction
Rosemary — for beauty
Sage — for purifying the body and environment
Sandalwood — to stabilize emotions and bring energy to new beginnings
Sweetgrass — for purifying the spirit

Try to contact other local groups of women who are doing these types of ceremonies, and combine your rituals on certain special occasions. It enhances the bond and it is a good opportunity to share chants, ceremony ideas, herbal combinations, and prayers. Most of all, stay focused, attain a positive direction, be consistent, and have fun! You will find that through repeated ceremonies the communal commitment will strengthen your personal goals and allow you to achieve a greater sense of self-worth and a lesser feeling of separateness.

The Moon Lodge ceremony is a good monthly reminder of our oneness, our connection, and the power we each have to improve our lives, our communities, and hence our world.

Afterword

Be still until the waters clear.
Do nothing until the darkness ends.
Rest until the storm clouds pass.
Wait for winter's breath to die.
Nature does not fight against itself.
Nor does it dance when the music ends.
— Ute

This time we are in is a time of intense healing. We have been awakened by a crying need that seems to belong to us individually; yet as we share with others, we find that same need crying from within them as well. We also affirm that the word "heal" comes from the same root as "whole" and "holy." Thus begins a paradoxical journey — a journey within which at the same time reaches out to all around us, All That Is.

Our teachers, the four-leggeds and wingeds, demonstrate for us a powerful healing way. I remember a time in my early childhood when one of our dogs came up missing. Four days later, he returned, weak, thirsty and thin, yet alive. It took little examination to see that he had been badly injured — a huge gash on his shoulder was the most evident wound. He had crawled off into a sheltered place of solitude and fasted four days. That stillness had powerfully begun his healing, which progressed rapidly as he began to drink and eat and move around again. Over the years I have observed many animals, both domesticated and free, practice this same healing technique. They instinctively know its power. We two-leggeds, as well, have deep knowledge of this healing way, although native peoples seem to be the ones who remember and practice it consistently. This gentle story, *Home Is The Heart*, speaks to us of the wholeness it is possible to achieve through such ritual solitude and other ceremony — a remembering of ancient knowledge.

New Age awareness has awakened many people to the wisdom of wholistic philosophies and practices that have been central to the healing ways of not only Native Americans, but other peoples around the world. It seems to me that in the primary (primitive) cultures, where there was little removal from the nurturing wisdom of Earth and Sky, there grew naturally a deep sense of connectedness, bondedness with all in the great circle of life. The events of the day, the creatures encountered, and all interactions were seen as profound metaphors for the deeper and the inner personal life.

In *Home Is The Heart*, a young woman realizes that death is not the central issue in her struggle with cancer — that the wholeness, meaning, and purpose of her life are crucial questions which she has neglected and which Death is calling to her attention. She is literally pressed to her belly on the Earth — to her center. "Bend with us, do not resist. Feel our Earth Mother beneath your belly. All things you need are within." Shamanic ways work with women to focus on their wombs, their bellies; here in this place where the miracle of life happens within them, lie incredible power and knowledge left untapped by the turning of our attention away from our bodies and reproductive organs in recent times.

The deeper function of the Moon Lodge (mentioned briefly in this story) is to participate in the visioning cycle naturally given women through their menstrual (moon) time, so that each moon brings a four-day period of fasting and visioning. The following elaboration on Moon Lodge practice is vitally important to women, especially in this time of PMS and female organ disease. This information speaks to the Feminine, the nurturing and renewing power within all, and calls especially to those who chose a female Earth body, for they express Grandmother's pull most eloquently. Your moon cycle determines the thinness of the veil between you and The Great Mystery.

The information received as the menses begins is the clearest human picture from within the womb of the Great Mystery, of the unknown and our future. Among our dreaming peoples, the most prophetic dreams and visions were brought to the people through the Moon Lodge. In other words, the most useful information that can come to us comes from each of you women who use your moon time well. Conversely, for each of us who do not honor this time, much is lost, including the respect of others for our bleeding. Dedicate yourself to the quest for vision that will guide us and our families at this time.

When your moontime approaches, pay closer attention to where you allow yourself to be, and to the energy around you, for you imprint very deeply during this receptive time. As the young woman here retreats into mountain solitude for healing, choose to immerse *yourself* in what you wish to receive, create, and magnify through yourself. Turn toward beauty, peacefulness, song, and vision for a radiant, harmonious life for your children and the children of seven generations. Refine the objects of your attention, until the blood comes and you retreat into the peaceful beauty of the Moon Lodge, leaving behind the everyday world for a few days.

During the days following the first clearing blood, whose potential for life we give back to Mother, the flow gentles, wanes, slows, and completes itself; we integrate the vision within ourselves and ready ourselves to come forth. The veil thickens as we turn from it, and we step into the present. We make ourselves solid, flex our lean bellies, and come forth. Grandmother's cycle within us assists us with the task of coming again fully present into the world. From the womb of

Buffalo Woman we carry new creations to join with the light, and birth takes place. This is self-transformation, and healing: our dream made real in the beauty of Mother's Earth.

This moontime practice, the vision quest/fast described in the story, and other forms of spiritual retreat are very vital to our lives, and they are frequently left out in modern times. Inner retreat and looking within are functions of the West on the Medicine Wheel — often called the Looks Within Place. The West symbolizes the quieting time of sunset, the releasing of outer forms as in autumn, and introspection. It is both falling leaves and harvest; and rather than being seen as an ending, it is understood as the place of beginning. We receive newness, begin again, not when our arms are full but when we have released the old, the habitual, the ordinary. In the West, we first receive the information and lessons that come from the activity generated in the South — we literally harvest. Then we practice letting go as in the dropping of leaves and seed-filled berries. We clean out and open up.

One of my finest teachers characterized this process by saying, "You can't smoke a cigarette and kiss at the same time." You must stop doing one thing before another can truly begin. So the harvested seeds and the compost of leaves are dropped into the fertile soil, where they lie dormant and still during the months of winter — North on the Medicine Wheel — where wisdom is achieved through getting down to the essence of things, the root of things, just as the plants demonstrate to us. From that crystal clarity and solitude comes the bursting forth of springtime, which is often seen as the beginning. Yet without the release of the old cycle, the wise dormancy of solitude, there would be no sprout, no new idea, no illumination in the morning light of a renewed cycle.

And so this young woman follows an age-old wisdom in retreating to the mountains, whose height and beauty have always represented for my people going toward the highest and finest we know — journeying toward the Great Spirit. She makes an outer movement to confirm an inner knowing, and thus strengthens her calling of Spirit into her life. The self-reflection made possible by her quiet life reveals much about herself that she had not touched before, as it will for any of us who will take the time. One challenge we instinctively know, which sometimes stops the less courageous, is that we will see much that is painful, displeasing, frightening; and yet the awareness gained from introspection is the first and giant step toward healing, because it is in our choosing to be blind to the truth that we stumble and fall.

And interestingly, it is retreat that brings her to community. In the mountain town, she discovers friends, both women of the Moon Lodge group and men of native spiritual lineage to give her added guidance, to deepen her experience through ceremony, prayer, and communion. And in her solitude as well, she begins to discover the community of the larger world: how her issues are the same ones facing the Earth and all its peoples at this time, that inner peace is essential in working toward world peace, and that the healing of herself is a piece of the healing of the world.

As well, she begins to understand that the cancer she carries reflects that disease of the Earth, the uncontrolled growth of human population which is eating the Earth and all our relations alive. Breast and uterine cancer begin to be seen as Mother Earth's inability to regenerate life and to nourish it. And the true cure, the real healing, cannot be topical only — dealing with individual issues of industrial pollution and deforestation — it must reach the source of the problem: our lack of good relationship with all other of Earth's children, no matter what their form.

Her cancer also reflects these relationship dysfunctions at other levels. She comes to terms with childhood patterning, such as her outward appearance as a "good girl" and her reality of emotional emptiness, despair, and family loneliness. She is made aware of the profound effect of her now almost unconscious decisions around the abandonment (by death) of her grandfather and fiance — her experience of the death of love and destruction of trust. "If she could handle the unfathomable anguish of the past, then everything else could be handled with grace." And although she felt that any new relationships must wait until she was cured, an unexpected, deep love for someone actually facilitates her recovery.

Another surprising love affair is deeply healing and produces a well of awareness and connection with other than human life. The owl she protects while it heals teaches her the balancing of mind, emotion, body, and spirit. The owl is a symbol of the ability to go through the night seeing and functioning well; and, of course, he helps her through her dark night of the soul. From his care she learns that "being responsible for (another being's) life was a sacred duty," and that she is as responsible for her own as she is for his. He might also symbolize death, another kind of night, which teaches her and then flies away, leaving her transformed.

This book portrays the dis-ease that many of us experience in our own lives in different ways, though not initially life-threatening; it shows that our deepest fears may indeed be of wellness; it gifts us fine reminders about the process of truly healing ourselves of any dis-ease: that we must first go within, and through our own transformation, heal the circle of life around us. As our young friend learns through her dream, each of us has all that we need within us:

"You must first unlock
the mystery of your heart.
We will guide you and show the way,
but you must do the work yourself."

So let us begin.

Brooke Medicine Eagle
Sky Lodge, Montana
15 December, 1988

About the Author

Roberta Gibson is a peaceworker. She believes that planetary, and hence universal, peace can only be accomplished by a distinct change in individual attitude and awareness. The primary focus of her service is to perpetuate this cause.

Mother of two, and a vegetarian for seventeen years, Roberta's work includes being a freelance writer and poet, sharing her spiritual source through words. She is associate editor and writer for *Total Health Journal*, and is working on her next book, *Heart Light*.

Roberta has been a certified massage/polarity therapist in private practice for eight years, utilizing healing techniques such as color therapy, chakra balancing, and reflexology. She is a state-credentialed teacher for the Colorado School of Healing Arts, and has participated in a variety of workshops geared towards enhancing psychic healing abilities.

A Colorado resident for nineteen years, Roberta develops and participates in many women's Moon Lodge ceremonies, and has studied other Native American rituals such as the Sweat Lodge and Yuipi ceremonies, and the Vision Quest. She has also been fortunate enough to witness a Hopi Snake Dance and a Sioux Sun Dance, and to be a foster mother to seven Sioux children for two years Her studies in shamanism and her personal experience with ritual have empowered her with spiritual strength and fostered a great respect for our Earth Mother.

Currently, Roberta is a staff member at Living From The Heart, a non-profit wellness organization that offers the "Dolphin Experience," an experiential therapy with dolphins. Through this service, the organization aids people in reducing stress, overcoming barriers, feeling joy and playfulness, and living from the heart — a big step on our planetary journey towards peace.